-Book Two of the Nevermore Series-

By K.A. Poe

An Original Publication Of FROSTBITE PUBLISHING

 A Frostbite book published by
FROSTEBITE PUBLISHING
PO Box 4435, Arizona City, AZ 85123

This novel is a work of fiction. Names, characters, and locations are either a product of the author's imagination or used in a fictitious setting. Any resemblance to actual events, locations, organizations, or people, living or dead, is strictly coincidental. No part of this book may be used or reproduced without written consent from the author. Thank you for respecting the hard work of this author.

Copyright © 2014 by K.A. Poe. All rights reserved.

ISBN-13: 978-1500488024
ISBN-10: 150048802X

Second U.S. Paperback Edition, 2014

Printed in the United States of America

Visit www.frostbitepublishing.com

For business inquiries, please contact Frostbite Publishing at fbp@frostbitepublishing.com

I would like to give a special shout-out to my younger sister Katee for sticking by me as a proud sister and avid fan and for urging me to write, write, write!

Also to my darling daughter Emily Poe, a world without her would be a world without magic.

And as with anything else, my husband Adam—I would never have come this far without you.

-Book Two of the Nevermore Series-

By K.A. Poe

Reflections

  As if being a vampire hunter hadn't been bad enough, there was also the dilemma of being in love with the enemy. Fortunately, he was nothing like the rest of them. He was gentle, more in touch with his human side, and feasted on the blood of animals instead of people. While that was comforting, I couldn't help but worry that something could corrupt him ... like it had my foster mother's boyfriend, who turned out to be a vampire. Like Salem, he was unwilling to feed on humans. That is until Janet cut herself one day and he lost control.

  Salem had been around me plenty of times when I was bleeding and never showed any interest, but that worry was always there. Then there was the other concern that I tried to ignore every time it slipped into my mind—what if I ever did something to hurt him? I was capable, beyond capable. It wasn't something that I would ever want to do, but I had powers that I couldn't completely control.

  The ability to become a raven was something that ran in my genes; however, it was rare. I was only the fourth Waldron known to possess the 'gift', as my father, Paul, called it. However, I wasn't quite to the stage of being able to do it at will. It most often occurred when I was around a vampire, or was in danger, and I phased easily in and out of shape. Paul thought the more I let it happen naturally the better I would be able to control it. Salem and I were both hesitant to attempt that, considering it would involve me being in danger. But, I finally felt ready to give it a shot, especially if hunting was going to become a regular routine in my life. The better I was at it, the less blood-sucking monsters there would be lurking around the world, and the less innocent people like Janet—my foster mom—would die. I could only imagine how many there were out there. Salem and his Sire, Raziel, had come from England before traveling to America. The thought made my mind whirl at the possibilities. If a few vampires could find their way into the quiet little town of Willowshire, then they could be anywhere ... everywhere.

That night I was to meet Paul and my aunt Kim in the cemetery—one of the last places I wanted to go. Less than six months ago, I nearly died there at the hands of Raziel. I was extremely lucky to have survived with just a fractured leg and a few scratches, as well as a very conspicuous mark on my throat that left an unsightly scar. Every morning I struggled to cover it with a layer of makeup, or ensure I was wearing a shirt or hoodie that hid the evidence. My leg had healed up nicely, and I was thankfully capable of walking without crutches after only a couple of months. If it hadn't been for Salem ... my mind whirled again at the possibilities.

I sighed and rested my head against the cool pillow behind me. I was alone in the massive canopy bed in Salem's bedroom. It was without a doubt the most comfortable piece of furniture imaginable. The mattress was plush, draped in ebony silk, and wide enough that I could spread out in any position I wanted—which, at that moment, was curled up in a ball worrying about the meeting.

Salem was out hunting, probably sucking the life out of a poor little rabbit in the forest beyond the large Victorian that I had begun to call home. It still bothered me, to some extent, that he had to kill innocent animals to survive, but I favored that idea over the unthinkable alternative.

As I laid there my mind began to reflect on the past eight months of my life—a life that had changed drastically. I had discovered my parents were not truly my parents. The man whom I thought was my uncle Paul for the past eighteen years turned out to be my real father. I learned that my birth mother had been slain by a vampire less than a year after I was born—the same vampire that had turned my beloved Salem. After this, Paul gave me up for adoption to Janet and Desmond Hobbs in the hopes of protecting me from the monster. He had only one condition, once I turned 'the appropriate age', which turned out to be eighteen by Janet's standards, the truth was to be revealed to me. Desmond and Janet weren't aware that this included the fact I was part of a lineage of vampire hunters, however. And then, I met Salem, a dashing, brilliant young man who turned out to be a vampire and apparently part warlock, which to begin with was something I couldn't quite accept, but I learned to adjust—especially after Paul revealed to me who and what I was.

Janet abandoned me to live with her new boyfriend, Mark, in Denver, who turned out to also be a member of the undead. Salem had insisted that Mark wouldn't hurt Janet, but it turned out he was wrong. I took a trip to Denver with Paul and Kimberly to make sure Janet was safe, but we were too late. I had lost the only mother figure I had ever known, and witnessed my first vampire slaying. That means both of my mothers, my real one and my foster one, were taken from me by the damned creatures. Salem was very lucky that he wasn't like the rest of them, or else he would be on my kill list. *I was fortunate.* During all of this, I had put off celebrating any holidays I had formerly loved. Halloween was a little out of my age-range now that I was eighteen, so I wasn't bothered with dressing up and going out for free candy regardless how tempting that was. Thanksgiving and Christmas came and went almost as if they were just ordinary days. Without Janet around, it seemed hardly like holidays could even exist anymore. Paul tried to make it feel festive during Christmas by bringing a few presents by Salem's house. He practically begged Salem to summon a fir tree and some decorations. We all hung the ornaments, and Paul draped the lights around the tree. Despite his efforts, however, it still didn't feel quite right, and I didn't believe it would ever again.

    I was suddenly pulled away from my memories when Salem peeked in through the bedroom door. He walked gracefully across the mirrored floor towards the bed, making me smile more with each step. He sat gently on the bed, and I tried to ignore the hint of crimson in his otherwise pale blue eyes—evidence that he had indeed found something to snack on. Knowing this made me uncomfortable; he attempted to avoid looking directly into my eyes.

    "I was hoping you would still be asleep when I returned," he said quietly, flattening the creases in the sheets.

    "Why?" I asked, watching his pale hands slide across the slick black material.

"To avoid you seeing me like this, and so I could lie with you." He looked at me once, briefly, to smile.

"I don't have to be asleep for you to lay with me, Salem."

"No, but you looked so comfortable and at peace." He smiled again and moved closer, cuddling up against me. I recoiled at first at the touch of his cool skin, then scooted back against him. "You seem distant Alex, is something wrong?"

"I was afraid you would notice," I grumbled. He always did. That boy could read me like a book, no matter how hard I tried to hide my thoughts or feelings. Part of me wondered if this was another of his mysterious abilities.

"What is it?"

"I was just thinking about the last few months," I murmured, "and about tonight."

"I'm not looking forward to it, either, Alex."

"I know. Will you be there?"

"Of course I will. Just in case ... "

After the close call I had last time, he wasn't very eager to let me go out alone. Paul and Kim didn't count as safe company, considering their past records. I was surprised either of them had lived through any of their hunting experiences with how bad their skills were—surprised, but thankful.

"Perhaps some breakfast will help clear your mind a little. It is the most important meal of the day you know." He winked.

"Sounds good." I smiled, knowing he wasn't actually going to cook. "Just something small is fine, scrambled eggs and sausage, maybe?"

"Deal." He grinned, kissed me on the forehead and hurried out of the room.

I stretched across the vast bed one last time before reluctantly climbing off and heading downstairs. Salem had summoned a plate with a small portion of scrambled eggs and two sausage links, which I ate hungrily as he stared at me from across the table.

"What?" I mumbled as I took a sip of orange juice and puckered. It was far more sour than I had expected.

"Nothing, I am just glad that you are here."

"Where else would I be?"

"Nowhere." He frowned. "You aren't the only one that has been dwelling on the past."

I put my glass down and sighed. "Salem, there's nothing to be worried about anymore. Raziel is gone; he can't hurt me."

"But he was close. Too close." I heard a faint growl escape his throat.

"No matter how close he was, he wasn't close enough." I slid a forkful of eggs passed my lips.

"I couldn't bear to live without you, you know." He looked at me, his expression serious and full of despair.

"I know." I reached across the table and touched his hand. "I'm fine, really, stop worrying about it."

"He's not the one I'm worried about anymore, Alex. There are more of them out there, more of them just as strong, if not stronger, than him. You cannot realize how many."

"And we will kill each and every one of them. I'm not helpless anymore," I said with a confident grin.

Salem simply shook his head. "This was a bad idea."

I impatiently waited for him to continue.

"You shouldn't be out there hunting. It's not safe. It is one thing to protect yourself if one comes for you, but to seek them out is crazy. Do you not remember how close I was to losing you last time?"

"Salem, you're the one who convinced me to listen to Paul in the first place ... "

"I know, and I was wrong!" He spoke harsher than I had ever heard before, but then his face went back to the concerned look he had before. "I don't want you to die because of me."

"I wouldn't be dying because of you. This would be my life, whether you were in it or not. With or without you, Paul would have seen to it that I became a hunter. It's in my blood."

Clearly, that didn't help. He looked even more upset by that fact. "I'm going to go for a walk," he muttered through clenched teeth. Before I could even protest he was headed towards the doors.

I stared after him, watching the large white doors slam shut. Pushing my plate aside, I contemplated following him but decided I should give him some space to think. Without the distraction of Salem, my mind began to race again about all that had changed. With an attempt to drown out the nagging thoughts in my head, I wandered into the living room and pulled out my well-read book of Edgar Allen Poe's works I had gotten for my last birthday.

It was mid-afternoon by the time Salem returned. He was withdrawn and uncommunicative no matter how much I tried to convince him everything would be fine. I wasn't used to seeing him like this. He was always in a good mood and open to discussion. When he came back into the house, he went straight to the white sectional sofa, and I immediately went and sat by him.

"Is there something you're not telling me Salem?" I asked quietly.

"I am just worried about you."

"That's all this is about?" I hated having to pry the information from him.

"Mostly," he finally said.

"You can tell me anything, you know."

"I know ... I just do not know if I can say what is on my mind right now."

"Is it about me hunting?" I asked, trying to figure it out without him having to say it.

"No."

"Is it about Raziel?"

He flinched. I must have been on the right track. "No, not exactly."

I swallowed before letting myself ask, knowing it would hurt him to hear it. "Hannah?"

"Yes." His voice was strained.

Hannah was Salem's half-sister. Raziel—formerly known as Thomas Winter before he became a vampire—was her true father. Salem only discovered this six months ago, and it was torturing him. His memory of being human was foggy, but Raziel had shared his own memories with him. He hadn't quite described the vision to me, all I knew was that Raziel had attempted to keep Hannah alive until it became too much, and he killed her.

"Salem ... " I said quietly, gently. "What exactly did Raziel show you?"

"That's really not going to help me feel better, Alex," he replied bitterly.

"You don't know that. Talking about things can help ... "

"He was at a house with Hannah. I cannot believe I was there, too, and unaware of her presence. How had I not known?!" He shook with anger. "She was probably six in the vision he shared with me. That means three years had passed since he took her. Three years during which I could have saved her. He showed me what became of her ... " His voice trailed off, and he sat up suddenly.

"What?" I asked, shocked by the bizarre look on his face. He looked almost hopeful. "Salem?"

"I don't think it was her, Alex."

I stared at him incredulously. "What do you mean?"

"The little girl he showed me, she couldn't have been Hannah." He shook his head. "Why would he want me to think he killed her?"

"I don't know what you are saying, Salem." My voice had grown concerned.

"It wasn't her! Her hair was wrong, her face ... her voice."

"She was older than the last time you saw her, Salem ... of course she was different. People grow; people change."

"No, this was not Hannah."

"How can you be so sure?" I frowned, partly wishing he would return to his state of despair rather than rambling on about seemingly nonsense and getting his hopes up.

"How could he possibly have kept her a secret from me during a course of three years? That would be impossible. I would have smelled her. I would have heard her. This was someone else entirely. It has to have been."

"She could have been kept somewhere else, Salem ... "

"Either way, I am almost positive it was not her!"

I sighed. "Then what do you think happened to your sister?"

"He would either have set her loose or … " he frowned, all sign of hope fading from his face, "…turned her into a monster like me."

"You're not a monster," I objected. "If he did turn her, wouldn't that be a good thing? It could mean she is still out there somewhere."

"But she wouldn't be the same."

"You don't know that, Salem. Maybe she would have turned out like you. Raziel showed me her, too, remember? I could sense good in her, pure goodness. I don't think a person like that can be so easily corrupted."

He smiled slightly at the thought, and then returned to sulking.

"Would you rather she have died, if this is all true?"

"No … maybe…I don't know." He sighed and looked through the window behind us. "We should probably get ready to go."

I glanced through the wide windows and noticed the sun had begun to set. That was my cue to leave. I begrudgingly left the comfort of the sectional and followed Salem out to my car. The Alero sat parked inside the garage. The car had seen better days and was now covered in blemishes of rust. The rain and snow over the years had beat freely on it without the safety of a garage until recently. We climbed into the old car and headed off towards the graveyard.

Control

    I was unsurprised to find Paul's Jeep Wrangler parked by the curb. I pulled up behind it and hesitated for a moment. Salem grimaced and exited the car, abandoning me for a moment while I gathered my crossbow from beneath the passenger-side seat. He wasn't comfortable at all with my use of the weapon, especially around him. He knew I would never hurt him intentionally, but one accident with the poison soaked arrowheads would be all it took. I tucked it under my hoodie and left the car.

    Paul was leaning against a street lamp; his arms folded across his chest and a bleak expression on his face. He was still uncomfortable with the relationship I shared with Salem, despite their apparent bonding after the incident with Raziel. Aunt Kim stood beside him—her face was the exact opposite of her brother's. She looked absolutely thrilled to be here, but that was no surprise for me. She worked as a journalist, but during any other hour, she was a thrill-seeker. That was her absolute passion. She told me numerous horrifying stories about parachuting, hang gliding, bungee jumping and swimming with sharks. Nothing, she said, was as thrilling as a vampire hunt, however.

"Evening," she said through her full, red lips. "Ready for some fun?"

I laughed, always amazed at her enthusiasm. "If that's what you want to call it."

"Paul and I are going to be behind you the whole way, but don't be surprised if we're out of sight," she replied, glancing once at her brother, then back at me. "We don't want them to know there's more than one of us out here if we can help it. Thankfully, the wind is blowing our way tonight."

My eyes widened. "*Them*?" I said hoarsely. Salem tensed beside me.

"I think we have at least two here tonight, judging from the stories we've been hearing."

"What stories?" I asked anxiously.

"Nothing you should worry about." She smirked. "All you need to do is stay focused and try to control your abilities. If things get out of hand, we'll be real close."

"This is a bad idea," Salem muttered. "One is bad enough. Going after a group, even if it's only two, is not smart at all."

Kim shook her head. "We can't just let them get away. Not to mention, the more danger she is in, the more likely she will phase."

"She's right," Paul intervened, uncrossing his arms and approaching me, "you'll be fine, and like Kim said—if things get out of hand, we'll be there. And so will he." He nodded toward Salem.

My stomach was churning as I slowly inched away in the direction of the cemetery gates. I glanced back to assure Salem once more that everything would be fine, but he had already vanished into the darkness. The air was unusually cool for May; my temptation to shiver was difficult to fight. With teeth chattering noisily, I slowly walked passed rows of old gravestones. How was I supposed to stop two vampires from noticing me if I was making so much racket? I stopped abruptly when I spotted them. They were leaning over what I could only assume was a body, pulled near an opening in the back fence. The unkempt and over encroached woods beyond nearly obscured them from even the bright moonlight.

    The male vampire was almost as bulky and tall as Paul. His back was toward me, but I was positive what he was doing. He knelt beside the head of the unidentifiable body. The person twitched and whimpered then ceased to move. I was too late to save them. Beside him was a short female vampire with long bushy black hair that contrasted her elegant snow-white skin. Her eyes were alert, and she was sniffing the air. I heard her whisper something to her companion, and he stiffened.

    I crouched low behind a nearby tombstone, knowing that within seconds he would be looking for the owner of this new scent. Peeking around the edge of the grave, I watched them creeping nearer. It was now or never. With crossbow in hand, I rolled out from behind the grave marker with full intent to let bolts fly. They were gone.

    "Too slow, little *hunter*." The male snickered. His voice came from behind me. Everything was already going wrong, as it always seemed to when fighting the undead. The girl was nowhere to be seen, but I ignored that fact—hopefully Kim or Paul would find her.

    My words failed me as I climbed to my feet and turned toward him. A lock of platinum-blonde hair dangled in front of his blood-red eyes. This wasn't going to be easy, but it never was. Paul had made it sound like a simple task when he introduced me to hunting—you go out, find the monster, shoot it in the heart, and you're done. However, there was always more to it than that. Tonight I was supposed to work on maintaining my transformation longer. Of course, the ultimate goal was to kill these monsters, but I was to do so as a raven. My crossbow was only to be used as a last resort. I had to keep myself and this vampire alive until my body altered ... however long that might take.

I swiftly dodged his first attack as he leapt at me. Despite my heart racing, the miserable feeling of changing forms wasn't happening, just as it had taken its sweet time in the fight against Raziel. He pounced again, knocking me off of my feet and slamming me into the side of a tree. I felt slivers of bark pierce the flesh of my shoulder. I knew the scent of my blood would send the brute into a frenzy, and if I was going to stop him, I needed to do it now. My crossbow had been knocked free from my grasp and lay mere inches from my fingertips. As the vampire pressed his strong hands around my neck, I dug my nails into his arm—it wasn't enough to distract him. My hand fell from his arm and dragged eagerly toward my crossbow. I could touch the back of it with the tips of my fingers, but it was no use.

Death was facing me once again, all because I couldn't control this damned 'gift'! He lifted me off of the ground with one hand, and then slammed me back down. A sudden rush of dizziness overcame me, ridding him of any resistance I had been giving. The platinum haired vampire lowered his lips to my throat and bit deeply. I cried out as the overwhelming pain raced through my body. Why wasn't the change coming?!

Before he had the opportunity to do much damage, he was gone. I heard a wretched crack and sudden *thud*! My eyes caught sight of something flying through the air. I sat up and saw the vampire pinned underneath a fallen tree, still as a corpse, and Salem glaring in my direction. Was he angry with me?

It only took a second for me to understand he wasn't looking at me, but at the woman behind me. He was there at once, knocking the bushy haired vampire to the ground with one touch. A monstrous snarl escaped the woman's lips, and she launched herself at Salem, barely knocking him back into a tombstone. I watched in horror as the movements flew by me, as if I was witnessing a movie in fast-forward—she hovered over him, her hands at his throat, prepared to snap his neck.

Finally. The crunching, unbearable twisting and curling of bones. The whirl of radiant feathers. I was flying. My beak opened wide and a harmonious, yet powerful caw whistled through the air. The female vampire crumpled onto the ground, grasping at her ears as the sound struck her. I avoided looking at Salem, knowing I was causing him just as much pain. I flew toward the woman and dug my talons deep into the flesh of her cold torso.

Without thinking, I pierced her lifeless heart with my beak. A cry of pure torture ignited from her throat, but I gave no mercy. I didn't stop until she fell limp beneath my body. Once I realized what I had done, I stared in shock at the vampire—the gaping, bloody hole in her chest. I turned my head anxiously toward Salem, who stood several feet away— his eyes were filled with horror. I stretched my wings, leapt off of the woman's corpse and fluttered in the air staring down at what I had apparently done.

Paul and Kim came out from hiding. They appeared impressed and satisfied with my work. But Salem ... I couldn't decipher the meaning behind his expression. Was he horrified by me? Angry? I couldn't look any longer. With one swift turn of my wings, I was off and soaring into the dark sky.

"Alex!" Salem's voice broke through the seemingly-endless silence. I ignored him and flew on. My wings flapped relentlessly behind me, guiding me away to an unknown destination.

Coward

    I felt like a coward as I soared through the darkness. This had been by far the longest amount of time I had kept shape, but that didn't matter to me right now. All that I cared about was the look I had seen on Salem's face when he saw what I had done. My wings carried me with no intended destination. It felt amazing to fly over the world. The cool rush of wind blowing passed me, the twinkle of street lamps below as I crossed over the highway. On-lookers would have thought I was just an ordinary bird. I flew until nothing looked familiar to me anymore.
    I spotted a tree on a nearby hill and landed gently on one of its many limbs. My eyes scanned the surrounding area. I could see cars in the distance, inching across the asphalt like baby turtles slowly approaching the ocean's edge as they fought to make it home. A large, luminous moon hung in the ebony sky surrounded by small sparkling stars. I couldn't make out any constellations across the sky, aside from the big dipper. That was as much as I knew about astronomy.

I contemplated returning home but the idea of seeing Salem right now somehow made me nervous. In an attempt to think of anything at all to clear my mind, I thought about Janet. It was still heart wrenching to think about her being gone for good, but this memory was more distant. I could see her and Desmond clearly in my mind's eye, laughing together as they pushed me on the children's swing. It was hard to believe there used to be a time when they were happy with one another. This memory had been enough to relax my body and mind; the adrenaline from the encounter was slowly wearing off. Just as instantly as before, the familiar feeling of bones twisting and cracking came, and before I could grip the branch in my new form, I fell to the ground. Everything went black.

When my eyes opened, I found the bright orb of the moon glaring down at me from between a jumble of tree branches. My head throbbed, and my back ached from the fall. I rubbed my eyes and sat up. Panic began to settle in when I became aware of the fact that I had no clue where I was. How far from home had I flown? Perhaps I would be able to shift back into the raven if I concentrated hard enough. Then maybe I could remember from which direction I had come. I doubted I could shift at will, never being able to before, but was there any harm in trying?

I sat still with my head between my legs, imagining myself as a raven hovering over the world. Nothing happened. I clenched my eyes tight, imagining the pain and discomfort of the transformation itself. Still nothing. This was pointless. Salem was probably worried sick, unless of course he was sickened by the thought of me—of what I could do to him. This was getting frustrating; I had been trying to learn to control this so-called gift for months. I slammed my fists on the cool ground in hopeless anger and let out a frustrated yell.

My body began to shudder. Snap. Crunch. Before I knew it, I was hovering through the air again, looking down on the spot I had just been sitting.

Without giving a second thought to how I had managed to shift I flew in the direction I had come. I had no idea how long the transformation would last this time, and falling from this height would be far worse than what had happened at the tree. Before I knew it, the cemetery was below me again, and I averted my eyes. The next time I gazed down I saw the trailer Paul lived in, the school building, the park. I couldn't be far from home now.

The vast white Victorian stood out among the thick foliage surrounding it. I hovered for what felt like a long time, wondering if I was ready to face him yet. I slowly lowered myself toward the back of the house. To my surprise, the window over-looking the lake was wide open and inviting. With one quick dive, I flew through the window and landed onto the sofa. I scanned the room quickly and was both disappointed and relieved that Salem wasn't anywhere to be seen.

My next step was to figure out how to phase back into my human form. If it was anything like it had been earlier, all I had to do was relax. That felt impossible. My mind was racing with all the possible outcomes from the night, and the adrenaline was still pumping through my veins from the race home. Maybe there was one solution.

I hopped off of the sofa and flew up the stairs and into Salem's bedroom. My reflection on the mirrored floor caught me by surprise, and I slammed head-first into one of the bed posts. Darkness swarmed around me once more.

"Alex?" Salem's voice was anxious. I couldn't decide if it was from fear or concern, maybe both. His cold hand caressed the side of my face, and I blinked my eyes open. His complexion appeared paler than usual, if that was even possible.

My head ached as I recalled the incident, but to my relief, my reflection was no longer that of a bird. The brunette-haired, hazel-eyed girl I saw every morning in the bathroom mirror gazed groggily at me. I scowled as I noted the red welt on my forehead and two small puncture wounds on my neck.

"Where have you been?" He carefully helped me up and sat me on the edge of the bed.

"I don't know ... " I mumbled. "Somewhere outside of town, maybe close to Silverton I guess..."

He sighed, staring at me without lifting his gaze for even a second. "I have been beyond worried. Paul has been calling every hour asking about you."

"I'm sorry." My apology didn't feel like enough. I felt ashamed, and hoped my tone made that evident.

"We waited in the cemetery for over an hour, expecting you to come back ... but you never showed up. Paul and Kim went home, but I stayed behind." He frowned. "Eventually, I decided to check and see if you had come home by chance, and thankfully, I was right."

"You didn't have to stay and wait."

"Yes, I did," he protested. "I wasn't sure if you were ever coming back."

There were no words to describe the way I felt at that second. "I was afraid that ... " I paused, "that you wouldn't want me to."

"Why in the world would I not want you to come back?!"

"Because ... the way you looked at me last night ... " I could barely speak.

Salem pulled me to his chest and held me tight—tighter than he ever had. "I was just shocked; that's all. You are so gentle and frail as my Alexis. Seeing you as the raven, doing what you did, I am still not used to it."

"You don't hate me? Or think I'm some sort of monster?"

To my surprise, he laughed. "This is coming from the girl in love with a *vampire*." His lips met the top of my head, and I melted comfortably in his arms. "Of course I don't think you are a monster, and I most certainly could never hate you."

"Good," I whispered. "I wish I felt the same."

He pulled my head up to look at him, "You could never be a monster, Alex." His eyes looked so sincere and gentle as he spoke, but I still felt unconvinced.

"I'm a monster for abandoning you last night."

"Alex, you didn't abandon me; you were just scared. I understand. Trust me."

As I lay my head against his chest for what seemed like a long time, a realization came into my mind. My eyes widened, and my mouth fell open as the fact hit that I controlled it; I altered shapes all on my own. "I controlled it Salem. I turned on my own…I…I don't know how exactly, but I did it."

He appeared curious but did not question me. He leaned back on the bed, pulling me with him. This was the perfect comfort zone, in his arms on his bed. I wasn't surprised to find myself dozing off slowly as he played with my hair and held me firm against him. It had been a long night.

Learning to Fly

    Paul was relieved to hear my voice when I called him the following morning and explained what had happened. He was overjoyed throughout the rest of the conversation, commenting on how impressed he was that I was finally learning to control the *gift*, as he always called it. I ignored most of his comments, although I did feel a slight sense of pride at my new-found skill. Thankfully, Paul didn't object when I ended the call early by falsely telling him I needed to eat breakfast.

    Salem was somewhat surprised when I rejected his offer for food, but I had other things on my mind. His eyes followed me curiously as I passed through the kitchen and into the living room. I stood in front of the sectional sofa, held my arms out at my side and focused my thoughts on something I truly didn't want to. The image of Salem being attacked by the female vampire played through my mind repeatedly. I could feel the sadness and anger building inside my core and my body began converting into the shape of the raven. I had found my source—Salem suffering, pain, anger, frustration—adrenaline. That would be enough to drive me into the wretched, deadly form.

My small, black head twisted backward to look at him. He was cautious, watching me flap my wings and rise into the air. If only I had discovered a way to speak in this form, it would make life much easier. I gave him a reassuring nod of my head and jumped through the window which was still open from the night before.

The wind whipped around me, threatening to blow me down with its force. I swam through the air, the breeze ruffling my elegant feathers. My reflection followed me as I hovered across the wide length of the dark water of the lake's surface. I lowered my body toward the water, letting my talons skid across its surface before rising through the air. To think I had once been terrified at the idea of flying in an airplane made me want to laugh. My body shook, and I could suddenly hear my voice screaming as I began to lose my focus. I was plummeting downward, my arms flailing at my sides.

I heard Salem's voice yelling from somewhere unseen before I was immersed in the cold water. I was fortunate to have been flying over the lake; I didn't even want to contemplate what would have happened if I had been flying elsewhere. Before I had the opportunity to get my senses straight, the panic was settling in. I felt the water seeping in through my nostrils. My eyes were wide with fright, until I saw something faint in the water. It was blurry and coming straight for me. My first instinct was to swim away, until it became clear what I was seeing.

Salem enveloped me in his arms and pulled me to the surface. I gasped and coughed when my mouth was out of the water. He dropped me delicately on the grassy shore and stared in disbelief.

"What were you thinking, Alex? You could have gotten yourself killed!"

My eyes, throat and nostrils burned. I coughed and spat out a mouthful of water. "It's not like I had planned to fall," I muttered.

"What *were* you planning then?"

"I was practicing ... and I was doing fine ... " I paused in an outburst of coughs, "until I started to think of something funny. Happiness, relaxation...it seems to break my hold on the form."

"Why didn't you warn me before you rushed out the window?!" His look of disappointment caused me to avert my eyes.

"I don't know, Salem. I was just thinking about how much Paul has been pressuring me to perfect this; I just want to be done already." I sighed, and then smiled. "But I have to admit, it is exhilarating, and I'm starting to figure it out."

"What exactly do you think about when you change?"

I grimaced and continued looking away. "Thoughts of you...thoughts of you in pain and suffering."

His expression was unreadable as he lifted me from the grass and carried me into the house. Rather than summoning me a blanket, he brought one down from his bedroom and draped it around my shoulders. It wasn't until that point that I realized how cold I was. After I finally stopped shivering, I accepted Salem's offer of a bowl of soup.

"Thanks." I smiled gratefully as he passed me a bowl of chicken noodle soup. He was pacing around the living room as I ate, which was awfully distracting. "What's wrong, Salem?"

He shrugged, not stopping his movements. "Hannah, you, hunting. Nothing out of the ordinary."

"You're going to drive yourself crazy if you don't relax, you know." I frowned and attempted to finish eating my food.

"Relaxing is no easy task when you are out nearly getting yourself killed on what seems to be a daily basis, whether it be to a vampire or water." His expression grew dark, and I sat my bowl aside. "As for Hannah, I cannot help but wonder if she is out there still. I know it is unlikely, and a large part of me sincerely hopes Raziel did not turn her. But I...I just don't know..."

"Maybe it's for the best if you don't know, Salem."

"I don't think so." He stopped walking and slumped over on the couch. "I wish there was a way I could know for sure."

"The world is a huge place; you know that even better than I do. Finding a single person is probably next to impossible."

"I know," he whispered into his palms as his head fell into his hands. "Make me a promise, Alex."

"Sure...anything."

He lifted his head and looked at me sternly. "The next time you decide to do that, please warn me ahead of time."

"I will," I whispered. How much shame was I going to be put through this week? "I'm going to take a quick shower."

I pecked him gently on the cheek and retreated to the bathroom upstairs. The steaming hot water trickled down my back as I sat upon the floor of the shower. There had to be some way to distract Salem from his thoughts of Hannah, some way to ease his worries, but I couldn't think of anything. There was no way I could call every Hannah Young or Hannah Winter in the country. And that was if she still went by that name. Not to mention that if she was still *alive*, it meant that she was a vampire. Who was to say that she had not become one of the bad ones? I know I had told Salem there was no way she could have been, but who really knew. Experiences can change people, even the gentlest of creatures can turn into beasts if they are prodded enough. If all this wasn't too much to mull over, there was the fact that the last time Salem had seen her, she was in England. I sat and thought for so long that the water began to get cold. I jumped up and shut off the water, draped myself in a towel, and dried off quickly. It was amazing how fresh, clean clothes felt after a couple of days of wearing the same outfit.

My feet hastily rushed down the spiral stairway, and I found my laptop on the dining room table. I had scarcely used it since Jason, my best friend from high school, gave me it on my last birthday. I felt bad for not having had the time to play with it as much as he had hoped, but it would be put to work today.

Salem was still sitting on the sectional, seemingly unaware of my presence. However, I knew he had to know I was there. He could smell me, no doubt. I frowned as I turned my head away from him and flipped open the laptop. My finger led the cursor to the Internet browser icon, and I waited as it opened. After I typed in a search engine's address, I hovered my cursor over the search box and typed in "worldwide obituaries". The screen was flooded with results, but I clicked the first one.

A white page came up on the screen with information on the website. I read down the page, letting the words sink in as my eyes slid passed them. There were empty text fields asking me specific questions such as first name, last name, birth, death, country, state of residency, and several other things.

I quickly typed "Hannah Young" into the name fields, followed by the year "1889" for birth and "1892" for death if she had died at the age of three. Once I hit enter, several listings came up—none of which appeared to be what I was searching for. There was one of a Hannah Young in Michigan, one in Canada, but nothing in Europe at all. I went back to the former page and put her name as "Hannah Winter" and came up with more unhelpful results. Next, I input both names with the date "1895", both of which came up with no results at all. If Raziel had killed her though, maybe her death would have never been known to anyone. Who knew what he may have done with the body? I shuddered.

"Salem?" I asked quietly, staring blankly at the web page.

"Yes?" he mumbled, barely audible.

"If your sister…" That got his attention, his eyes were now fixated on me. "If she had died in the fire, there would be an obituary, right?"

"Right. There are rarely obituaries made without a body, or any large amount of evidence." He was obviously curious. "But I told you she was taken out the window by Raziel; I know that now thanks to the vision he shared with me."

"I know. Do you think if Raziel did…if he," I paused, not eager to say what I knew would send hurt into Salem's heart at the spoken words, "if he had killed her … would there be any chance of an obituary?"

"Doubtful. Raziel couldn't have really told anyone about it. Having a young girl in his possession that had supposedly either died or went missing during the fire would have aroused too many suspicions. No, vampires, for the most part, live a very cautious existence." He stood up, and in a matter of seconds was sitting on a chair beside me. "Why do you ask? What are you doing?"

"I was just thinking about what you said, about Hannah. I was doing some research and there are no obituaries for her anywhere," I replied, then typed in "Arthur Young" and browsed through the listings. I immediately found his file listed on the site. "Your father is on here, and I am willing to bet Maggie is, too. Of course what you said makes sense. Even if Raziel had killed her, she probably would not be listed. I'm sorry Salem; I tried."

"As monstrous as he was, I know he loved her. Even if he had lost control and killed her, I have little doubt he would have buried her. Alex, I know there are records of graves in general. Those done by funeral services, but also those done by families on their own accord and that are eventually found. It was not uncommon in those days for a family to bury a loved one themselves; many places had their own small cemeteries. Would you be able to search for that, on this?" he gestured towards the laptop.

I typed "Grave Records" into the search. Plenty of results came up, but nothing looked like exactly what we needed. One of the link names did give me an idea for another search though, and I quickly punched in "Find a grave". I went to the first result. The site was exactly what I needed; similar to the obituary you could enter information and get details on where a grave was located. Many of them even had pictures. I once again entered Hannah's name, leaving all else aside from the birth date blank. No results aside from the now somewhat familiar Michigan and Canada graves. I tried again with the alternate last name; the loading bar felt as though it would never finish. Finally, the results page popped up—it was blank. There were no gravestones recorded that matched Hannah's information.

"So, she might still be out there ... " he whispered thoughtfully, "or it may just be that her grave was never discovered."

"But it does give us some hope, right? She *could* still be alive, somewhere. The odds of no one finding and reporting her body or grave in over a hundred years seems pretty slim to me. Doesn't it to you? If she is still out there though, I have no idea how in the world we could find her." I scowled. Even though I had used the word 'hope' for Salem's sake, I had truly wished I would have solved the problem by discovering she was indeed dead—as terrible as that sounds, it would have at least put Salem's mind back at ease. That is what he had always believed until recently anyway. Instead, I opened up a whole new can of worms. I half expected Salem to jump up, ready to go on a hunt to find her at any moment.

Salem smiled at me, which was not the demeanor I had expected at all. "Knowing that she might still be out there is enough for me."

"Are you sure?" I asked, bewildered. Did he really not intend to search for her after all this worrying?

"Of course. I know there is little chance that I will ever see her again, but knowing that she might still exist ... that at least makes me feel somewhat at peace."

"Wait," I mumbled as a thought popped into my head. "If he turned her, would that make her a blood-thirsty three-year-old for all eternity?"

Salem arched a brow and laughed. "No. Humans that young are physically incapable of being turned, which means he would have to have kept her alive somewhere until she was at least pubescent."

"Does that make you upset?" I asked cautiously.

"No ... It is relieving that the vision he shared with me about Hannah's death could have been false. Only created and shown to make me suffer. It means that he did not want me to know the truth, for some reason. It makes me more curious than anything else."

My mouth opened to ask him what he thought of the possibility of her having turned out like Raziel. What if he had kept her around much longer than Salem had even imagined? What if he had raised her to be as he was? But I stopped myself. "I'm just glad to know you are fine with all this now, and we can put it behind us again."

"Right," he said. Something in his voice made me feel as if that was far from the whole truth.

"You have a voice mail, by the way," he said, thankfully changing the subject. "It's from Karen."

A Normal Life

After listening to the message from Karen, I gave her a call back and unintentionally made arrangements to meet her the following afternoon for lunch with her and her cousin. I was seriously dreading it. Thinking about it, I couldn't even recall the last time I spent time around someone who didn't know my secret. It wasn't going to be easy to be around them, but once Karen brought up the idea of going out for lunch the words were out of my mouth before I had the chance to think it through, "I'd love to."

"Do you want me to join you?" Salem asked after I hung the phone up.

"Karen wants it to just be us girls." I sighed. "I think I'd rather be out fighting vampires than being a 'normal girl'."

Salem laughed and hugged me comfortingly. "It will be just like before all of this happened. You will ease back into the routine."

"I doubt it. What will I even talk about now? I spend all of my time either with a vampire or hunting one!"

"Make something up," he suggested.

"Sure," I grumbled. "I'll tell her I've been on vacation or something." I hated having to lie to my friend once again, but I didn't know what else to do.

"They will probably believe it." He smiled reassuringly. "Just try not to think of me suffering. I wouldn't want for you spontaneously turning into a bird during your meal."

My eyes widened in horror. I hadn't even thought about that possibility. Salem had said it in jest, but the reality of it was that it could happen.

Salem saw the look on my face and knew what I was thinking before I even spoke. "As I said, avoid those thoughts and you will be fine." He kissed my forehead and hugged me tightly. "Everything will be great. You will have fun."

"I hope so ... " I said, still shocked at the prospect of accidentally transforming before my human friend. "I think I'm going to go ahead and go to bed."

"I will be there shortly." Salem smiled as I released myself from his embrace and wandered upstairs.

Sleep wasn't coming easily. Even now that Salem was beside me, I simply couldn't fall asleep. I pretended to be unconscious, however, because I didn't want him to be concerned. I tried to count sheep, to count backwards from one hundred to one, but the main thing that dwelt in the back of my mind was the possibility of phasing in front of Karen and her cousin. Why had he had to bring that up? Living a "normal life" again seemed impossible. Maybe it was a mistake to have told Karen I would go. Then again, maybe the mistake had been choosing to live this secret life. I was thrust into it, but I still made the final decision.

Before I knew it, the sun was up, barely visible behind the black curtains framing the wide window across the room.

I grumbled and rubbed my eyes. At some point I had finally dozed off, but my body felt as though it had never slept. Salem was still beside me; his eyes shut although he wasn't asleep. Slowly, quietly I raised my head over his and stared at his peaceful face. Strands of ebony hair fell across his pale forehead. I brushed them away gently with my fingertip before kissing him delicately on the lips. I gasped as he opened his eyes and a smirk played across his face. He pulled me tight against his body and pressed his lips hard against mine. When our mouths parted, all I could manage to do was smile.

"Good morning," he mused and kissed me once more.

"It's off to a good start," I commented, taking his cold hand in mine. "I'm not so sure the rest of the day will be as great. Ugh. Promise me everything will be all right at lunch with Karen?"

"I promise, but it's not something that I have control over," he replied and tightened his grip on my hand. "You will be fine, Alex."

"Thanks..." I half-smiled and reluctantly climbed out of bed. I retreated into the shower, hoping to wash away the feeling of exhaustion. It helped somewhat, but I knew the relief wouldn't last. I dressed in a loose-fitting light blue blouse and a black knee-high skirt.

Salem stared at me as I came downstairs. "I take it you like my outfit." I laughed when I entered the living room, sashaying about mockingly.

"You look lovely," he replied. "You will fit in perfectly among a group of regular girls."

"That's the plan." I smiled and was distracted immediately by the small bowl of strawberry yogurt sprinkled with granola on the dining room table. "Is that breakfast?"

"I figured something light would be best, so you have plenty of room for lunch."

"How thoughtful," I replied genuinely and began eating. The sweet, creamy texture of the yogurt went perfectly with the crunch of the granola. "I don't know why but this is so good!"

"I'm glad," he said from across the table. "If you don't mind, while you are away, I think I would like to test out your *laptop*."

"Of course I don't mind." It was somehow odd picturing Salem using a computer. He wasn't entirely thrilled with the idea of technology, for whatever reason. "What did you want to do with it?"

He shrugged. "I haven't quite decided yet. There are so many things that the device can do, it is amazing."

"I guess you're right," I replied, took my bowl to the sink and rinsed it out. I suspected it had more to do with Hannah, but I didn't want to stir anything up for now.

My thoughts were preoccupied with the view laid out before me. I was resting with my head against my crossed arms as I leaned over the back of the sofa. My eyes were admiring the landscape outside Salem's house—something I had never quite taken the time to fully enjoy. With how the white paned windows framed the magnificent view, it was almost a surprise that I wasn't staring at a painting.

Tall, dark mountains arched upward in the distance, clouds casting shadows upon the rocky surfaces. Trees surrounded the area from every direction. Most of them were covered in lush, brilliant green leaves. Where there weren't trees, there were berry-speckled bushes, boulders ranging in various sizes, and a wide field of green grass that danced in the breeze. Although I had nearly drowned in its depths twice now, the most captivating piece of this scene was the vast lake.

I could barely make out the trail that led through the dense forest and toward the clearing. I mostly focused on the rippling of the dark, blue waters as my eyes slowly fell shut and sleep washed over me.

"Alexis?" Salem said, nudging my shoulder gently. "You're going to be late."

The temptation to ignore him was difficult to resist, but I raised my head and rubbed my eyes. "Thanks," I replied groggily. "I guess I didn't sleep too well. I should probably finish getting ready…"

I ran upstairs, brushed my hair, put on some light make up and tugged on some socks and shoes. As I was leaving, I hugged Salem close and kissed him gently. "I'll miss you."

"Not nearly as much as I will miss you," he replied with a simple smile. "Call me if anything happens."

"I will," I replied and headed out the door.

Karen called me not two minutes after I got into the car and refreshed me on the directions to the place we were meeting.

I pulled into the parking lot of what appeared to be a typical, small cafe. The building's exterior was all brick, painted in a deep espresso color—very fitting for what the business was. Coffee was just what I needed to wake me up after the restless night before. When I came to the front of the building, I discovered an arched beige door with a sign dangling from a bronze hook above. The sign was in the shape of a coffee cup, and it read in an elegant script: *'Kaplan Kafé '*. The café appeared to be newly built, which was somewhat surprising for such a small town. Even more amazing was the crowd I discovered upon glancing through the windows. Amidst the many people, I spotted Karen sitting at a booth beside a strawberry-blonde haired girl who I'd never seen before.

A gentle chiming bell sounded when I pushed the door open, alerting the lady behind the counter that she had a new customer. It also caught Karen's attention, who immediately waved me over when she saw me. I smiled as I walked over to the booth and sat across from the two girls.

"Hey, Alex!" Karen said and grinned. "I hope you don't mind, but I went ahead and ordered for you. White chocolate cappuccino, right?"

"Yep, you know me too well." I grinned in return, inhaling the strong scent of coffee lingering in the air. It was only partially true—there was no way for her to know me very well these days.

"Well, I'd hope so by now," she said, and then glanced toward the girl sitting beside her. "This is my cousin, Claire."

I finally set my eyes on the strawberry blonde girl who sat beside my friend. Her hair was in short, dangling curls that perfectly framed her rounded face. From her overall appearance, I would have guessed that she was around sixteen. She had wide, vibrant topaz eyes. Something about her felt familiar, but I couldn't quite place what it was. "Hey Claire. I'm Alex."

"Hello," she replied. Her voice was sweet, almost musical. "Karen has told me a lot about you."

"Oh, really?" I said curiously as Karen got up to retrieve our beverages.

"Yep. She told me that you guys have been friends since before she can remember."

"That's right, and we even used to be neighbors; that's how it all started," I replied thoughtfully. It was bizarre thinking how much time I had spent with Karen throughout my childhood, and now I seldom spoke to or saw her. I had to admit, I was enjoying being among a "normal" crowd again already.

Karen returned and sat down a tray with three 24oz Styrofoam coffee cups on it. Each cup had a name written across it in thick black ink—Alexis, Karen, and Claire. I grasped the one with my name on it, took a sip and gagged.

"Way too hot!" I gasped. "I can't believe I just did that."

"Well, it *does* say 'Caution: Beverage is hot' on the lid, y'know." Karen laughed and shook her head as she slid back onto the booth.

"I guess I just haven't had coffee in a while." I chuckled uncomfortably, and my cheeks grew warm.

"It's been a long time since you did a lot of things," she mumbled in response.

"What's that supposed to mean?"

"Just that you've missed out on a lot. I was really shocked when I heard that you dropped out of school. Jason was the one that told me; it would've been nice if you had maybe told me beforehand," she said sadly.

Claire sat idly beside her, gazing out the window. "I'm so sorry, Karen." I sighed. "Things haven't been very normal for me lately."

"I understand. I was just surprised; that's all." She smiled reassuringly. "Are you still living at Paul's house?"

I went to correct her by saying I had never stayed with Paul, but then remembered that was the story I had given Jason when I told him he could live in my house for free. "Oh, no. I'm not."

"You're not living with Jason and Mitch, are you?" I could hear the jealousy in her voice. It still felt strange that she was interested in Jason.

"No! I can't imagine what that would even be like ... all of the parties he would have going on." I shook my head. "I'm staying with another friend."

"Another friend, huh? Who?" she asked, finally taking a sip of her latte. I could sense that she was somewhat annoyed that I had not asked to stay with her, although she tried to hide it.

I didn't reply right away, as I sipped my cappuccino and pondered if I should even tell her about my living situation. "Do you remember that boy I met in music class last year?"

Her eyes changed dramatically and she grinned, "You're living with him?!"

I felt my cheeks grow warm again as I fought the urge to smile. "Yes."

"Oh my god! Did he drop out of school, too?"

"No. He wasn't even enrolled in school, actually. Janet," I paused after saying her name, it still hurt to think of her, "I mean mom, had him find me to tell me something important."

"Oh. What's his name?" I was already beginning to regret mentioning it; I knew she would never stop asking questions now.

"Salem." This time I couldn't hold back from smiling.

Claire glanced at me; she almost appeared alarmed. "Did you say *Salem*?" she asked.

"Yeah, why?"

"That's a very weird name," she replied. "What's his last name?"

"Young," I replied, somewhat cautiously. "Do you know of him?"

I couldn't quite read her expression—it was a mixture of shock, hurt and satisfaction. "No ... I don't," she mumbled. "Karen, I think I have to go."

"But you have barely touched your drink!" Karen objected.

I hadn't noticed Claire touch her beverage at all. "Take it with you," I suggested, trying my best not to think too deeply into the matter.

"Yeah, sure…" she said with an attempted smile as she grabbed her cup. "It was nice meeting you. Really."

Karen and I stared in awe as she walked out the door. This didn't distract my friend for very long; her eyes were once again on me. "So, tell me more about him!"

I laughed and began telling her about Salem—how pleasant he was, about his interests in music and history, how he wanted to travel the world, that he was born in Wales, and that we were practically inseparable. She grinned the whole time, taking in every word.

"He sounds amazing, Alex!" she said once I finished droning on about him. "When do I get to meet him?"

I blinked, not expecting that response. "Wow. I don't know. Maybe we can make plans to do something together."

"I'd love that," she was back to grinning. "You're… you know ... together, right??"

"Right," I said, mimicking her grin. A rush of butterflies fluttered through my stomach. "What have you been doing?"

"I just got a part-time job at Howard's, thanks to Jason recommending me to the owner." Her pride was obvious in her tone, but I couldn't blame her. "We work pretty much the same shifts, so we get to see each other all the time now, just like school."

"Is there anything going on between the two of you?" I said with a sly smirk.

She frowned. "No. I think he has his eye on somebody else."

"Oh," I groaned, worrying that he was still stuck on me, "that sucks."

Karen shrugged and sucked down the rest of her latte. "I'm glad we're still friends at least, though. My car broke down about a month ago; he offered to drive me to work and back until I can afford to have it fixed."

"That's good. About him driving you, not about the car breaking down," I said. "Who knows, maybe all that time you two are spending together may spark something!"

"Maybe," she said hopefully. "It was nice seeing you, Alex. We should really get together more often…like we used to. And I am especially anxious to meet this boyfriend of yours!"

I blushed again. "Right. We'll have to set something up on one of your days off, maybe."

"Well, I'm off this coming Friday, so just let me know," she said with a wink as she left to dump her cup in the garbage.

"I'll have to ask Salem what works for him first, too, can't make plans without letting him know," I said, secretly hoping he would say no.

"Great! Well, I need to go get some new clothes for work." She grinned at the sound of her words. "Want to come with?"

"Sorry, I can't," I mumbled, staring down at my cup as I tried to come up with an excuse. "Salem and I already had plans later today."

"No problem," she replied. "Have fun. Call me when you figure that out about Friday!"

"I will."

"And Alex…"

"Yes?"

"Let's never go that long without seeing each other again, okay? I miss you. Jason misses you."

"I know. I'm sorry it's just that lately…"

"I know. Salem. He's obviously important to you, Alex. Just don't let him make you forget about us."

"Never."

She smiled half-heartedly and headed out the door.

Claire

For roughly ten minutes, I sat at the lonely booth sipping the last bit of coffee that remained in my cup. I hadn't even noticed the annoying sucking sounds I had begun to produce until an older lady in the booth in front of mine cleared her throat and gave me a nasty look. I sent her an apologetic smile, dumped my cup and headed through the arched doorway. A welcoming warm breeze brushed against my skin and rustled my hair. My feet led me to my Alero, but I stopped in shock when I reached it.

"Claire?" I muttered, finding her leaning against the back wall of the café. She was eying me suspiciously as I inched closer to my vehicle.

"Alex," she answered with an unexpected coldness in her voice. It didn't sound quite as musical now. "I was hoping I would catch you out here. Didn't expect to have to wait so long, though."

"Oh...I was just finishing my coffee," I replied. "Did you need something?"

"I just wanted to thank you," she said, the melody coming back into her tone. I stepped away some as she approached me. "Don't worry; I don't bite." She laughed a little and rolled her eyes.

"What are you thanking me for?" I asked, obviously confused.

She was mere inches from me now. The wind blew the scent of vanilla from her skin all around me. With one swift, delicate movement, her hand was on my shoulder. I wasn't sure if I had imagined it, but I was certain I felt an electric jolt flow through me at her touch. "I wanted to thank you, for being there for Karen." She gave me a warm, friendly smile.

"Oh," I said awkwardly. "I haven't really been there for her much lately, though." A pang of guilt ran through my entire body once again.

"I know, but every little bit counts, and I do appreciate it." She smiled once more, a slight dimple forming in her cheeks.

"Oh, well...no problem. I love Karen like a sister. Was that really all you wanted, though?"

"That was it. I'm sorry to hold you up; I'm sure you're busy." Her hand lowered from my shoulder, and she stepped away. "I hope to see you again soon."

"Yeah, you too ... " I whispered and quickly climbed into my car. As I was pulling out, I spotted an empty Styrofoam cup and a puddle of caramel liquid beside the building—I could barely see the black ink across the side of the cup, but I was almost certain it said her name. Claire's topaz eyes were locked on me the whole time as I left the parking lot.

I hastily ran towards the front doors of the Victorian as a sudden downpour fell from the sky. It took me just seconds to get to the door, and I was already soaked. Salem was sitting at the dining table when I entered, his face hidden behind the screen of my laptop. He peered up over the top of the device and frowned at me.

"You are drenched," he said.

"Thanks, Captain Obvious," I replied, a little harsher than I had intended.

"Captain who?" he said, looking a little confused.

"It's just a saying...never mind. I'm going to run upstairs to change out of this mess."

After pulling off my soggy clothing, I dried off quickly with a towel and pulled on some fleece pajamas. I was back in the dining room within ten minutes. Salem hadn't moved an inch. I pulled up a chair beside him.

"What have you been doing?" I asked, eying the laptop curiously.

"I have been struggling to find answers to Hannah's whereabouts," he replied sheepishly.

"I thought you had given up on searching because it was practically impossible."

"It's not easy to give up." He sighed and shut the computer gently, then reached his hand out to touch mine. "Did you have a good time?"

I shrugged. "It wasn't as bad as I thought it would be. Karen sort of wants to meet you ... "

"There is no harm in that." He smiled. "I hope you didn't spend the whole time rambling on about me."

"Pretty close." I blushed and looked away. "I'm just glad that there wasn't anything to make me turn."

"I told you there was nothing to worry about."

"Yeah...something weird did happen, though,"

Salem looked uneasy. "What happened?"

"Karen's cousin was acting kind of bizarre," I replied. "When I mentioned I had a boyfriend she immediately got up and left. Then, I went out to my car and she was standing there waiting for me … she said she just wanted to thank me for being in Karen's life. The weirdest part was when she touched me … it was almost like a bolt of electricity went through me." I shuddered as I recalled the feeling.

"Maybe the subject of significant others is a tender one for her, you can never tell. Although the rest does seem a little odd," he replied. "What was her name?"

"Claire," I shrugged. "She didn't give a last name."

"Had you ever met her before? You had told me that you and Karen were inseparable as youths, did she ever mention this cousin?"

"Not specifically, but her family is spread all over the place. She's mentioned cousins plenty of times, but I don't think she has ever named names. It's probably nothing, but anyway…I am starving. I thought we were going for lunch, but it was just coffee. Can I have some lasagna or something?" My stomach had begun growling ferociously.

"Of course," he replied with a pleasant smile, and I watched his eyes glow violet temporarily. A plate with a square of lasagna on it appeared before me.

"Thanks," I said gratefully. "If I'd have known she had just meant coffee I would have definitely had something more than just that little bit of yogurt for breakfast."

"Coffee," Salem said with obvious disgust, his nose wrinkling, "one of the worst smells there are."

I laughed. "I guess it would smell awfully strong to you." I began eating the meal Salem summoned for me. It was warm and delicious. "This is better than any lasagna I have ever had!" I commented between mouthfuls.

"I'm glad you are enjoying it. It was hard work." He flashed me a bright smile and retreated quietly to his shelves of books. As I ate, I watched him sit on the armchair beside the bookshelf. He was deeply engulfed in whatever he was reading, completely unaware of my watchful eyes.

After consuming my square of lasagna, I dumped my plate in the trash. I laughed quietly to myself when I imagined what it would be like if Salem kept every dish I ever used. The counter tops would be stacked to the ceiling with them! He didn't appear to notice me as I walked passed him and curled up on the sectional. My mind was filled with memories of this afternoon.

There was something unsettling about the way Claire had behaved. Part of me hoped I was making something out of nothing, but another part of me knew there was something going on. I sat up and stared out the window at the moon as it lingered above the lake, casting a magnificent silvery reflection against the watery surface. My thoughts grew depressing as I considered how many nights Salem had spent on this planet, compared to how little I was going to have. How many nights had he spent staring up at the sky in all its glory? He could sit through an entire sunrise and sunset without losing a second of his life. I was going to grow old and weak, while he maintained the same flawless, youthful body he was trapped inside forever. I wasn't sure what had brought on these thoughts or feelings, but they were persistent...and saddening.

I shut my eyes, feeling a tear trickle across my cheek. Had he ever considered this? It was frustrating how he could so easily read my expressions when I rarely knew what he was feeling or thinking. Maybe this was why vampire and human relationships never worked out; I mused. When I felt confident that my tears had dried, I turned to glance at Salem.

"I'm going to bed," I said, my voice cracking towards the end.

His eyes narrowed as he looked away from his book. "Is something wrong, Alex?"

I shook my head and faked a yawn. "I'm just really sleepy."

Salem looked unconvinced and set aside the novel. "If something is bothering you, you should tell me," he frowned when he sat beside me and noticed the faint lines left from the moisture on my cheeks. "You have been crying."

My eyes lowered. "I was hoping to avoid this."

"What were you hoping to avoid exactly?"

"Talking to you about what is on my mind," I mumbled.

He stared at me impatiently. "Tell me, Alex, please."

"Someday … " I paused, knowing if I spoke any further I would start bawling. "Salem, someday I'm going to be old and brittle. I won't stop aging."

He reached across the sectional and cradled my face in his hands and smiled—how could he smile after that? "If only you knew how much of a gift that really is."

"Gift?! I'm sick of that word. This isn't one of those 'the grass is greener on the other side' kinds of things, Salem. Don't you get it? If I don't get killed hunting vampires or something first, I will eventually die of old age!"

"It is better than being this cold, husk…this monster. I would gladly-"

"Right, I know. You would gladly be human if you could, blah, blah. We'll see how you feel when I'm some wrinkled up old woman, and you still look eighteen." I wasn't sure where all this was coming from. Perhaps it had been building up in the back of my mind. As harsh as it was, it was still all true.

"Alexis, I will always love you no matter what. And when you are gone, so shall I be."

This wasn't helping. "Or you could just turn me! We could be together forever."

"No! You don't understand what you ask of me. Trust me; one normal life is better than an eternity like this."

"Whatever, Salem, forget I brought it up. Let's just go to bed. I'm exhausted."

Nightmares

    The cool blankets beneath me did not compare to the feeling of Salem's cold chest. Even through his shirt, the chill radiated outward, cooling me from the warm summer night. Suddenly he pressed his lips hard against mine. I struggled to breathe under the pressure, when he finally pulled back I gasped for air. Before I had even fully taken that breath, his lips traced the edge of my jaw, lingering at the base of my ear for a mere second before brushing across my neck. My eyes grew wide as I felt a burning, stabbing pain rising against my throat. I gasped and tried to push him away but he wouldn't budge. He was too strong. What was wrong with him? I screamed and cried as the burning increased. I could feel my blood, no, my entire essence being beckoned out of the holes pierced into my neck.

    "Alex!" Salem yelled, and I could feel him shaking me awake. "Wake up, Alex!"

    I pried my eyes open, staring wildly at him through the darkness. My hand instinctively wiped across my throat. There was nothing there. I sighed with relief and stared at him cautiously.

HYBRID

"Are you all right? You have been flailing around and whimpering ... I could barely get you to wake up!" His voice seemed very concerned.

"Yeah...I'm fine. Just a nightmare," I muttered and jumped off of the bed. "I'm going to get a glass of water."

"Do you want me to summon it for you?" he offered as I inched toward the door.

"No ... that's okay."

Frowning, Salem sat and watched me walk out into the darkness. My attempt at going steadily down the stairs failed as I shook uncontrollably. With each lift of a leg, I feared I was going to tumble down the rest of the steps. Fortunately, I made it down safely. Although the house was pitch black, I had become accustomed to its layout and could easily find my way to the kitchen without bumping into anything.

I froze as I went to reach into one of the cabinets, wondering if I would even find a glass. To my surprise, there was a singular cup sitting on the lowest shelf of the chosen cupboard—I wondered if Salem had summoned it there for me, or if it was coincidental. Then I reminded myself that he once told me there were no coincidences. Holding the glass in my unsteady hand, I slid it under the faucet and let it fill up with cold water. The moisture against my lips was soothing, but the images from my dream still fought their way to the surface.

This was the first nightmare I had experienced in at least ten years, aside from the dream I had after Salem told me the story of how he became a vampire. I suffered from them occasionally as a child, but never throughout my teenage years. With my glass firmly clutched between my fingers, I walked through the darkness toward the sectional and sat down. Part of me feared the very idea of attempting to sleep again. That same part of me feared returning upstairs to Salem's room.

Without really thinking about it, I set my glass of water against the coffee table and curled up on the couch. I stared blankly at the half-empty cup and tried to think of happier thoughts. I began to realize I didn't have very many of those. The happiest memories I could conjure were my eighteenth birthday when Jason brought me my much unexpected laptop, and the night at the creek when Salem told me we were "twin souls"—that we were meant to be together.

A wide smile crossed my lips as I shut my eyes and relived that moment. I scarcely noticed Salem slink down the stairs and sit beside me on the couch. He hesitated, and then gently pulled me close to him. I nuzzled against his leg as I drifted off to sleep once again.

Claire stared at me from across the clearing, a radiant crimson hue to her eyes. Her complexion was as white as cotton, a mischievous grin played across her lips. I was standing across the log-bridge over the creek, balancing myself steadily when I noticed her startling appearance. As I gasped in shock, I could feel my body tilting to the side.

"You do not belong here." Her melodic voice was harsh. "Leave Salem alone and go back to your normal life. He *will* hurt you, whether you believe it or not."

My balance returned temporarily as I crouched down on the fallen tree. "Salem wants me here," I objected.

Claire leapt forward, jumping straight across the clearing in one bound. She was at the base of the creek, a low growl emitting from her throat. "I do not believe that for a second. Vampires don't want humans in their lives."

"How do you know he's a vampire?" I asked.

She shook her head, strawberry blonde curls bouncing elegantly against her shoulders. "Raziel told me you would try this. But I won't let you!"

"Try what? I don't understand ... " I whispered fearfully. "Where is Salem?"

"He is right behind you." Her lips curved upward into a horrible grin as I turned around. Before I had the opportunity, I could feel the cold lips against my throat. A burning sensation ran through my veins as his fangs sank into my skin once again.

"NO!" I cried, lifting my head up and staring around the room. My heart was racing, and I felt like my breath was caught in my throat.

Salem was still beside me, immediately enveloping me in his arms. I wanted to fight it, to escape, but I couldn't. "Calm down, Alexis," he whispered soothingly into my ear as I sobbed against his shoulder. "Was it another nightmare?"

My head barely moved as I nodded; I wondered if he could feel it.

"Would now be a bad time to ask what these have been about?"

I mumbled against his shirt, telling him detail after detail about both dreams I had. He tensed somewhat as he listened, mostly during the parts where I mentioned him hurting me.

"That's never going to happen," he said comfortingly, holding me tightly. "They're just dreams."

"They are not just dreams; they are nightmares...worse than nightmares. They are so real," I said quietly, my voice barely audible through the sobs. "Why was Claire in them, of all people?"

"You just met her; she was fresh in your mind. Maybe you were just thinking about your coffee house visit before you dozed off," he suggested.

"No. I was thinking about you."

"I don't think it is anything to be concerned about. Dreams are strange things that do not necessarily mean anything."

"This coming from the boy who never sleeps," I grumbled and tugged away from him. "I don't think I am ever going to be able to sleep again."

"Of course you will. You can't *not* sleep."

"You could make it so I never have to," I whispered, wishing I could take back the words as soon as I said them.

Salem looked disappointed and sighed. "Alexis we just talked about this, please don't tell me you are still wanting...*that*."

"If I did, I'd be lying." I frowned.

"I told you before, Alex … nothing is worth this kind of life. Not even me." The last words stung.

"Oh … " My lips trembled and I swallowed hard. "I-I think I'm going to go out for a while."

"What?" His eyes narrowed and he reached out for my hand, which I quickly moved out of his grasp. "It is barely five in the morning, Alex! Where would you even go?"

"I don't know...someplace...normal."

I watched him open his mouth to speak, and then slowly his lips creased into a thin line. "If you don't desire to be here … " his voice trailed off, and he avoided looking at me, "I won't make you stay."

The wet tears cascaded down my cheeks once more as I turned away from Salem. I grabbed my car keys and cell phone and was out the door before I could even give myself the chance to reconsider. The trees surrounding the

Victorian swayed around in the strong breeze that was building up. As I crossed the path on the way to the garage, I could only picture Salem sitting there on the couch sulking. I was making him miserable, but it served him right. Was I really asking so much? How could he say he loved me but not want us to be together in this life forever? I kicked the side of the garage hard in frustration.

My voice shrieked in surprise as my body contorted and the whirl of feathers surrounded me. *Not now, not now*, I thought pleadingly. The keys and phone I had previously held now lay on the concrete.

Hovering over the land, I heard the door fly open as Salem came out—no doubt alarmed by the sound of my scream. I glanced down at him through my beady black eyes, and the disappointment and pain painted across his pallid skin sickened me. I turned and flew from the scene, ignoring his calls after me.

Home

    My wings beat noisily behind me as I pushed through the heavy gusts of wind. Rain began to trickle down from the gray clouds, and I could see faint evidence of the sun shrouded behind them. I had one place in mind that was safe, normal, and I would be accepted easily without too much questioning. The rain grew heavier, and it was becoming difficult to fly through. As I neared my destination, I had to come up with a way to calm myself.

    My talons clicked gently against the roof of my former house. This place was filled with so many memories, one of which surely would be comforting enough that I could relax. The first thought that came to mind was the morning I discovered Janet had left for Denver. Following that memory was that of my eighteenth birthday, which was somewhat relaxing but at the same time a nuisance. I climbed down from the roof and landed gently on the mowed lawn. Knowing Jason was taking care of the place was a reassuring thought.

    I fluttered across the lawn, noting Jason's car parked on the gravel driveway. There was scarcely any evidence that a teenage boy was living here. Not only was the lawn well kept, but the windows weren't smudged, the pathway to the front door was swept, and the trash cans were pulled to the edge of the sidewalk for pickup this morning. That was enough. My mind was clearing of negative thoughts. I heard the sickening crunch, felt the brutal twist of bones, and within seconds I was standing upright on the lawn.

I approached the familiar red door with the tiny peephole and hesitated. It was early. Jason was probably asleep and he probably had work today. What was I thinking? Shaking the thoughts loose, I rapped my hand against the door. Perhaps he wouldn't be too upset by my sudden appearance.

Time ticked by slowly as I awaited a response. No one answered, so I knocked again. I heard movement beyond the walls and knew I had succeeded in waking someone. When the door opened, I was surprised by who answered.

"Mitchell!" I gasped. Of course. Why wouldn't he be here? I told Jason his brother was more than welcome to live at the house also. He looked hardly any different from the last time I saw him—his thick, curly brown hair was slightly longer, there were obvious signs of exhaustion on his face, and he had lost some weight. Mitchell had always been skinny, but now he was too skinny.

"Hey, Alex," his voice was strained, and he wobbled slightly as he leaned against the door. "What are you doing here so early?"

"I was hoping to see Jason," I replied. "Are you all right?"

"Yeah, just really tired," he laughed. "I had actually just fallen asleep. They have me working the late night shift over at the diner."

I groaned quietly when I recalled my last visit to the diner. "I'm so sorry I woke you up. I can leave if you want me to."

"No, don't be crazy," he smiled and welcomed me inside. "The place is technically yours, anyway."

When I stepped in I couldn't help but notice the place was practically the same as when I had left it—at least in terms of furniture. The same faux leather love seat, the same dull scratched up coffee table, and the same dining room table. I felt comfortable here; I felt at home. The sink was piled up with dishes, but I really couldn't blame the boys—they both had jobs to worry about, and Mitch had a few more weeks of school before summer break. The sofa had a blanket and pillow strewn across it, leading me to believe that was where Mitchell had been asleep.

"You don't have a bed?" I asked as I walked through the dining room.

"You know I do, but I just hardly ever sleep in it," he shrugged, "by the time I get home, I sort of just slump over on the couch and pass out. Then a few hours later I'm up for school. I do nap in the bed after school though."

"That's terrible," I frowned. "Are you and Jason struggling to pay the bills or something?"

"No, we have that covered," he grinned and sat on the love seat. "I'm saving up to buy my own car."

"Oh, awesome!" I thought about when I got my first car as I glanced around the house. A bundle of dirty laundry lay beside the edge of the love seat. "How close are you to being able to buy it?"

"Maybe another two weeks of this. But it will be totally worth it!"

I laughed and hesitantly sat beside him on the love seat. "Is Jason asleep?"

"Yeah, he should be up soon, though," he commented, glancing at the alarm clock set upon the end table. I recognized it immediately with a pang of anguish—it had been Janet's. "He usually gets up around 7:30 or so."

"Do you care if I wait around for him?"

"Of course not." He glanced at me and frowned. "You look just about as tired as I feel, Alex."

"Yeah ... " I mumbled. "I haven't been sleeping well either. That's kind of why I came here, to get away from my troubles."

"Things not working out between you and Salem?"

I blinked, wondering how he knew about him. "Did Karen tell you about that?"

"Um, you've met Karen, right ... ?" He laughed. "As if she could keep her mouth shut about anything!"

"Yeah...I guess you're right."

"Jason didn't take it too well."

I was afraid he would say something like that. "Why not?" I asked, acting like I didn't know.

Mitchell laughed, harder than I expected. "You're as blind as Karen is loud! You really didn't know all these years? Jason has had the biggest crush on you forever!"

"I didn't know until a few months back, actually," I admitted. "It still surprises me."

"There's nothing not to like about you, Alex," he said with a wink. "Even I had a little crush on you when we were younger, but unlike Jason, I grew out of it. Good thing too...he didn't care for the idea of someone else liking you." He laughed.

I stared at him in awe. I wasn't that likable, was I? Maybe it was just the small town, not much variety. "That's flattering," I said uncomfortably. "But anyway, there's nothing wrong with me and Salem ... I just needed to get out, and he was asleep," I lied slightly.

Mitch nodded his head in understanding. "Well, you're always welcome to stay here, y'know. If for some reason you can't or don't want to go back to his or something."

"Thanks," I murmured.

As Mitchell opened his mouth to speak, I heard noises coming from upstairs. "Who are you talking to?" Jason's voice called down the stairs. I was relieved to hear him; it had been far too long.

"Oh, you'll see," Mitchell replied playfully.

"You didn't bring a girl home with you last night, did you?"

"No, she sort of just showed up on her own." Mitchell smirked at me.

Jason rushed down the stairs, obviously curious to see who the mysterious girl was that his younger brother was with. His face sank as his eyes fell upon me, sitting beside Mitch on the love seat. "Alex ... what are you doing here? And what are you doing with Mitchell?"

I sprang up from the seat. "I wasn't doing anything *with* Mitch!" I laughed nervously. "We were just hanging out while I waited for you to get up."

"Oh, right. Okay." His expression softened. "That still doesn't tell me why you're here."

I shrugged. "I didn't know where else to go."

"Are you ... " he paused, "are you and that guy having problems?" He sounded almost hopeful.

"No, we're fine. I just needed to get out for a bit, and to see you," I added in the last part in the hopes of relieving him.

"You look exhausted." I stiffened as he came closer and pulled me into a hug. "And you're soaking wet!" he exclaimed, pushing me away gently.

"Oh ... yeah," I muttered, barely even aware of the fact that I was drenched in rain water.

"Did you walk here or something?"

"Something like that, yeah."

Jason shook his head and plucked his brother's blanket from the back of the sofa, draping it around my shoulders. "Wouldn't want you getting sick." He smiled.

"Thanks," I said, returning the smile. "Do you mind if I hang around here for a little while? Maybe I will even clean the place up a little." I chuckled.

Jason laughed—it was a pleasant, familiar sound. "You don't have to do any cleaning, but we'd love it if you stayed."

"I want to clean," I objected, glancing around at the clutter again. "You'll thank me later."

"Sure," he replied. "It's only going to end up like this again in a few days, though."

"That just gives me more to do."

"Are you avoiding something?" he said with a frown, all amusement washed away from his face.

I shrugged. "Kind of. I have been having these really disturbing nightmares lately, so I'm trying not to sleep."

"That's healthy," I heard Mitchell mumble from the sofa, upon which he was now curled up with his face toward the back of the couch.

"It's hardly any less healthy than what you're doing!" I shot back. "How much sleep have you gotten in the past few weeks?"

"Not enough," he grumbled.

"See, so shut it." I smiled jokingly at Jason.

Jason took my hand unexpectedly. "Come upstairs with me," he offered.

I eyed him suspiciously. "Jace, she still has a boyfriend, remember? No funny business." Mitchell snickered, and Jason shot him an angry look.

"I just wanted to show her what we've done with the rest of the place."

"Suuure you were."

"Let's go," I said, partly just to get away from his brother's comments, and followed him upstairs.

Jason led me across the familiar creaky floorboards. To my immediate left was the singular bathroom, which had been kept almost exactly as it was when I had left it—besides the addition of their toiletries. Ahead of us, down the hall was Janet's old bedroom. Her bed, her dresser, everything that had belonged to her was gone. I stared throughout the room in disbelief. In place of the large bed with frilly pillows that I remembered so vividly was a twin-sized bed with plain dark-blue covers. A shabby brown nightstand sat beside the bed. Where Janet's dresser had been was a different, shorter one that I was unfamiliar with. Socks and other assorted clothing items poked through the crease between the drawers of the dresser. My eyes were drawn to a picture frame on top of the dresser.

"Wow," I whispered, picking up the frame and running my hand across the glass surface. The picture was of three children—a round-faced, blonde-haired girl with radiant green eyes stood to the left, in the middle was a chocolate-eyed boy with a broad smile and a head of deep brown hair, and beside him was another little girl with long brunette hair, hazel eyes and a toothy grin. "This picture has to be ancient."

"It's not that old," Jason said with a chuckle. "What were we, like six...seven?"

"Probably," I replied. "I miss those days."

"So do I. Life was a lot simpler back then."

I laughed; he had no idea how much simpler it was than my life these days. "What has become of my old room?"

"You'd never know it had ever been a girl's room; that's for sure," he replied and led me down the hall to my former bedroom.

I gasped at the sight of it. There was clothing everywhere! I couldn't make out a single inch of the familiar dull gray carpeting underneath all the laundry. The walls were covered in posters of scantily dressed women lying on cars or motorcycles. Shaking my head, I turned and left the room. I couldn't bear to look at it anymore. "Here I thought, with how clean the lawn was that the inside would be just as tidy." I laughed dryly.

Jason looked apologetic. "We've both been really busy, Alex."

"I know," I replied. "I understand completely."

"Shouldn't you be leaving to get Karen?!" Mitchell yelled from downstairs.

"Yeah!" Jason shouted back, and then looked at me. "Sorry, I've got to go. But I'm so happy to see you again, Alex."

"It was good seeing you too," I said earnestly.

"Will you be here when I get back?"

"That all depends on when you'll be back," I replied.

"Pretty late."

"Then probably not."

He frowned at me and embraced me again. His skin was warm and comforting. "I've missed you."

Without thinking, I wrapped my arms around him, returning the hug. "I've missed you, too, Jace."

"Promise you'll come back soon, okay?"

"You know it," I said and smiled.

We both walked downstairs. Mitchell was turned over on the sofa, facing us with a wide grin, and kept raising his eyebrows up and down. Jason smacked him playfully on the shoulder. "I'm just messing around, lover-boy."

"Well, stop it," Jason replied coldly. "See ya later, Alex."

I watched him grab a coat and keys and slip out the doorway. Mitch sat up on the sofa and rubbed his eyes. "'bout time for me to get ready to go, too."

"Are you serious?" I asked in shock. "You must be miserable. You should call in sick."

"Nah, I'm used to it." He smiled reassuringly. "I'll be in the shower if you need me."

I was all alone downstairs in the place I used to call home. My eyes cast upon the laundry pile beside the love seat. I lifted the heap in my arms and walked through the kitchen, down a short hallway and into the utility room where the washing machine and dryer were located. Plopping the mass of discarded clothing into the washer, I poured in some detergent and started running the wash. Next, I went to tend to the dishes.

Mitchell found me in the kitchen washing the dishes and looked at me in shame. "You don't have to do that, Alex."

"It's fine; I want to do it. Anything to keep me busy and awake," I said as I ran a plate through the stream of water. "Don't worry about it."

"If you say so," he said quietly. "I'm going to walk to school."

"Okay," I replied. "I probably won't be here when you get back."

"Well, it was nice seeing you!" he said and draped an arm around me in a half-embrace.

"It was nice seeing you, too." I smiled, but he couldn't see it. I listened as the door shut behind him and returned to washing the remaining dishes. After the dishes, I spent the next ten minutes staring inattentively at the TV set until I heard the washer stop. I sluggishly wandered into the laundry room, moved the clothes to the dryer and went up to Mitchell's room to gather even more clothing.

The more I did, the harder it was to fight just how tired I was becoming. I was down to two loads left by 9:30. Mitch's bedroom was flawless, and I was satisfied. I sat on the edge of his mattress and glanced around the room. It felt like so long ago that I had slept on a different bed in this same room. My body took control and I was suddenly on my back, staring at the ceiling and dozing off.

My vision was blurred, but I could make out shapes around the room. Two figures stood against the far wall, toward the bedroom door. They muttered something incomprehensible. One of them came closer to my body. I attempted to move, but with horror, I realized I was paralyzed. A cold hand swept across my cheek, and I could faintly make out their face. Salem. His face looked different. It wasn't the gentle, sweet face I was used to seeing. He looked fierce, blood-thirsty.

"Kill her, Salem." The voice was unmistakably Claire's. "Her blood is irresistible to you. Don't fight it any longer." Her voice was hypnotic, even to me.

I wanted to scream, to tell Salem she was wrong, that he didn't want this, but I couldn't move my mouth. All I could do was lay there and wait for him to kill me. He hesitated a moment as he stared into my eyes, then his lips were at my throat again. I could scarcely feel the burn or the stab.

I shot upward on Mitchell's bed, clutching a pillow to my chest. My heart was thumping loudly, and it took me a second to realize I was being watched. *Please don't be Salem,* I thought as I turned to see who was sitting in the corner of the room on the computer chair.

"Jason?" I blurted out. "What time is it?!"

"Almost six," he whispered. "Are you okay?"

I shook my head. How could it be six? "I don't know ... "

His face displayed a look of confusion, and he cautiously sat on the bed beside me. "You have been whimpering in your sleep," he said sadly. "Crying, too, I think."

"Why didn't you wake me up?!" I shouted and smacked him with the pillow.

"Hey, relax!" He tugged the pillow away. "You were exhausted; I figured a bad dream was better than waking you up."

"Well, you were wrong," I grumbled.

He shifted uncomfortably on the bed. "Alex ... can I ask you what the nightmares have been about?"

"You wouldn't want to know." I laughed coldly.

"Sure, I would," he said, resting a hand comfortingly on my shoulder. I fought the urge to shrug it away.

"To put it simply ... they've all been about Salem trying to kill me." It was painful to say the words.

Jason looked bewildered. "He's not hurt you, has he?" he asked, looking me over as if scanning for bruises or cuts.

"No! They're just nightmares. I don't know what has brought them on."

"They just started last night?"

"Yeah, they started after I met up with Karen and her cousin, Claire ... " I hated speaking her name. Even though I didn't have a solid reason to dislike her, these nightmares were making her seem like an enemy. "She acted really weird after I told her about me and Salem."

"Claire? I don't remember Karen ever talking about a cousin Claire before."

"Weird, maybe they were never close until recently," I mumbled. "You guys spend like, every minute together at work, right?"

"Close enough," he agreed.

"Jason, could you do me a favor?"

"Anything, Alex." He sounded almost too eager.

"Can you drive me home?"

"Yeah, sure."Hhe was obviously reluctant now. I wasn't certain if he believed me about Salem not being abusive.

𝕿𝖊𝖒𝖕𝖔𝖗𝖆𝖗𝖞

I sat with Jason in his car, parked just a few feet away from Salem's house, for what felt like hours. This had been the second time I had abandoned him—this time with even less reason than the last. With a quick sigh, I pulled the car door open and climbed out. Jason followed behind me, uninvited. Considering what I had put him through, I opted not to say anything and let him come with me.

"How in the world did you even manage to walk from here to my place?" he said in awe as we walked up the alabaster stairs.

"That's a story for another time," I mumbled.

As we approached the front doors, Jason eyed the stained-glass windows and glanced at me. "What's this?" he asked.

"Art." I shrugged, not about to give him the full details behind the bat and the raven etched into the glass. "Salem made them."

Should I knock or just walk in? I couldn't make up my mind. Fortunately, I didn't have to. The doors flew open and

Salem stood inside, at first he appeared relieved and then somewhat furious when he noticed Jason beside me.

"C-can we come in?" I muttered, feeling somewhat stupid.

Salem arched a brow. "You don't have to ask to come into your own house, Alex." He stepped back, allowing us entrance.

"I know ... " I said quietly as I stepped over the threshold. "Salem, this is Jason. Jason, Salem."

Neither of them seemed to acknowledge the introduction. I sighed. Jason appeared just as amazed by the interior of the house as I had during my first visit. Salem looked distraught as he watched me walk into the living room and flop onto the sectional. I knew by the way he glanced at Jason that he wished he wasn't present.

"I'm sorry," I mouthed.

"You probably guessed by now, but Alex stayed over at my place," Jason said as he stopped marveling at his surroundings. "She was really upset."

"I know," Salem said in a surprisingly calm tone. "Has she slept at all?"

"Yeah, that's why she was gone so long," Jason explained. "She woke up during a nightmare, though."

"Another one?" I stared at the anguish that was displayed on his beautiful face, "There must be something I can do to stop them." He appeared to be talking to himself more than to either of us.

"She seems to think not sleeping will work," my best friend responded, shaking his head. "I let her sleep through her last dream, and she got mad at me."

Salem grinned. "Good of you to let her rest, however. I am thankful for that."

My eyes darted back and forth between the two of them. Had they forgotten I was even here? Jason sat beside me on the sectional and placed a hand on my shoulder. "Thanks for cleaning up the house, Mitch and I really appreciate it."

"Anytime," I mumbled. "I guess I'm thankful that you let me sleep, even if you were letting me suffer!"

"You were dreaming, not suffering." Jason laughed. "I'll see you later, Alex."

"Thanks for driving me home," I said with a grateful smile.

"Take care of her, okay?" he said to Salem as he walked toward the door.

"I will," Salem promised.

Once we were alone, Salem sat on the sectional. He was clearly hesitant to sit near me after my outburst from the previous night. I scooted across the couch until I was beside him and wrapped an arm across him. My eyes stared apologetically into his, and he managed a faint smile.

"I am so sorry Salem, really," I said with a pout. "I was being stupid."

"I am just glad you are back."

"So am I." My head rested against his chest. "I wish I understood why you keep killing me in these dreams."

He didn't reply.

"Salem ... " I said, lifting my head and looking at him again. "Jason said he has never heard of Claire before, even though Karen is around him all the time ... and you know how she is with gossip and stuff. You would think she would have mentioned her by now."

He appeared deep in thought as he listened to me. "That is odd."

"Is there any chance that she could be a vampire?" I asked suddenly. "She is one in my dreams."

"Does she look like a vampire?"

"No ... She looks like a normal girl," I replied. "Her skin is tan, her cheeks rosy. There's nothing undead about her appearance at all."

"In that case, I do not believe she is a vampire."

"Well, there's something off about her."

"Perhaps," Salem replied thoughtfully. I watched his eyes glimmer purple for a mere second, and a dish materialized on the coffee table: ice cream. The same thing he used to calm me the previous time I was feeling depressed. Aside from sleeping, food was the last thing I wanted right now. "It's chocolate," he commented, "and you must be starving."

With a sigh of defeat, I leaned over and plucked the bowl from the table. "I really don't feel like eating right now, Salem."

"You'll feel better if you do," he insisted.

I stuck the spoon into the moist, rich cream and put it to my mouth. To my surprise, there was a swirl of caramel throughout the ice cream that tasted amazing. "Caramel," I said with a smile, "my Kryptonite."

"I thought you might enjoy it," he said with a grin.

And I did. I felt much better than I expected after consuming the dessert. Cuddling up against Salem's cold body, I yawned sleepily. I couldn't believe I was still tired. "Tomorrow is Thursday," I mumbled.

"Yes," he replied, stroking my hair gently. "What is your point?"

"We have to make arrangements with Karen to get together on Friday."

"We can worry about that tomorrow."

"Well, I *am* comfortable." I chuckled and shut my eyes, temporarily forgetting my fear of sleep. Salem kissed the top of my head lightly as I drifted off.

When I woke up, I was surprised to find myself cuddled up against Salem in his bed. My memory was foggy, but I was absolutely certain I had fallen asleep on the couch. Slowly, the grogginess faded and I lifted my head from my pillow and glanced at Salem, who was staring out at the bright sun. The curtains had been drawn open, and a radiant glow was filling the room. The satin sheets appeared to sparkle as the light shone across the bed. I squinted my eyes and sat up.

"Good morning." Salem smiled when he noticed I was awake. "You slept peacefully."

"I did!" I said with a look of surprise.

"You must have been exhausted, considering you didn't stir even the slightest when I brought you up here."

I laughed. "I was pretty sure I hadn't fallen asleep up here."

After a quick breakfast of eggs and toast, I dialed Karen's number on my cell phone, which hadn't suffered too much damage after being dropped on the sidewalk the other night. My friend answered immediately. She rambled on about various ideas she had for things we could do—see a movie, go out to eat, get coffee again—all things that I couldn't picture Salem enjoying at all. Out of the blue, I suggested she come over to our place and we could have a picnic beside the lake. Karen was more than thrilled at the thought of not only meeting Salem, but seeing where we lived.

As I hung up with Karen, another call was coming in. Paul's name shown across the screen of my cell phone, and I considered ignoring it, until Salem insisted I answer.

"Hello?" I said, trying my best to hide my eagerness to get off the phone.

"Hey Alex. Kim and I have a target in mind for this evening, if you were interested in joining us."

This had been the exact reason why I was hoping to avoid talking to him. After the last hunting experience, I wasn't at all keen about the idea of going ... ever again. But, in a sense, it was my destiny to protect the world from the undead.

"Fine," I grumbled into the receiver. "When and where?"

"Actually, this might be a bit shocking, but it's not in the usual place." His voice was calm, but I could sense something behind it. Worry, perhaps. "It's down by your old house."

I nearly dropped the phone. "What! Is Jason okay? Mitchell?"

"They're both fine. There have just been bizarre sightings. We aren't even sure it's vampire related, but thought it would be wise to check it out."

"What kind of bizarre sightings?"

"I guess people have been seeing a girl snooping around the place. Jason called the local police department to report the sighting, as have a few other neighbors," Paul explained.

"How do you get a hold of this information, anyway?"

"I heard it first on the police scanner."

"Aren't those illegal unless you are a cop or something?"

"Well, I also heard it again from your aunt, she's a journalist, remember? When she isn't off on assignment she writes for the newspaper," he reminded me.

"Oh, right," I mumbled. "This was serious enough to get into the paper?"

"No, but she still hears the little news reports around the office, and I bet you anything they have a scanner or two also, legal or not. Anyway…we'll meet you there around 7:00 tonight, okay?"

"Okay," I replied. "See you then."

I hung up the phone and relayed both messages to Salem. He wasn't overly concerned about the call from Paul, as there currently was no proof that it was a vampire or anything else harmful—for all we knew, it was some girl from school trying to sneak into Mitchell's room. That wouldn't surprise me. As for having Karen over tomorrow, he seemed a little uneasy about the idea.

"It won't be any different than us going out someplace with her," I said.

"I am more concerned at the thought of her bringing Claire with her. I don't want that to spawn more nightmares for you."

I shrugged, although I doubted myself as I spoke, "She probably had nothing to do with it."

"No, but she was involved in most of them. Seeing her might trigger them to return."

"Seeing you hasn't triggered them," I said matter-of-factly, satisfied at the dumbstruck look on his face.

"You're right," he replied simply, then glanced away from me. "Alex, would you like to go for a walk?"

"Are you asking if I want to join you while you go hunting?" I replied.

"That might also be involved with it, yes."

"Well, let's go," I said, took his hand and followed him through the back door.

Despite the sunshine, the air had a slight chill to it. The creek was over-flowing with water from the recent downpour. The dirt that aligned it had become thick sludge. I watched in disgust as Salem willingly advanced through the mud as I stood idly behind him. He shot me a look as he walked through the water, perfectly balancing on the rough, obtuse rocks.

"Are you coming, Alexis?" he asked as he almost seemed to walk across the water. How did his feet not hurt from walking on those stones? "If you are afraid of the mud ruining your shoes, take them off."

"It's not so much that as I just don't want it on me!"

He looked at me again with a playful smile upon his lips. "Do you not realize that once you get passed the mud, your feet will be submerged in water ... which will clean away the mud?"

I grimaced at his flawless face, knowing he was right. "Fine, but what about when I have to walk back through it on the way home?"

"I'll carry you," he suggested. "Come on. It's not nearly as cold as last time, I promise."

With a heavy sigh, I wobbled as I stood with one foot and plucked off my right shoe and sock, then the left. I cringed as my bare feet sank into the brown mush. The worst part was feeling it between my toes. Eagerly, I stepped into the creek and washed away the debris. The water was shockingly warm as I wriggled my toes beneath the clear surface.

"I told you it would be fine," Salem said as he watched me.

"Yeah, yeah," I mumbled. "It feels really nice."

I peered upward; the sun hung high above us in the clear blue sky. Brilliant rays crept through the canopy of leaves above, spreading sunshine across the land. Salem's pale skin was more defined in the sunlight, but it didn't surprise me—I had noticed it once before.

"Are you going to go hunt down a bunny or something now?" I asked, somewhat mockingly.

"I had something else in mind, actually," he said, gazing off into the woods.

"As long as it's not me," I mumbled.

His laughter was pleasant and he quickly embraced me in his arms. The cold of his skin made me shiver despite the warm water beneath me. I lifted my head to look at him, admiring the way his eyes seemed to shimmer in the daylight. I was momentarily distracted by the feel of his lips against mine—cold yet invigorating. I hungered for more, but he pulled away. He appeared distracted by something.

"Stay here," he said, slowly releasing me. "I'll be right back."

"Where are you going?"

"There's an elk nearby." His answer was simple, but I understood completely.

"What about bunnies and squirrels?" I laughed.

"Elk is more filling." He shrugged. "Just, stay here, okay?"

I nodded, noting the urgency in his voice. "I'll be here."

In silence, I watched him fade into the thick foliage. Awaiting his return, I knelt over the rippling creek water. Beneath and betwixt the large slate rocks were small, colorful pebbles. I reached down and gathered a few in my hand, held them up in the air and dropped them back into the water. Smiling at the interesting sound they made at they hit the surface, I grabbed another handful and went to drop them until something caught my eye.

    The sunlight cast upon something in the clear liquid. Whatever it was, it glinted and shone brightly. I leaned forward to get a closer look. It appeared to be a thin golden chain. My hand dove into the water after it, gripping it tightly between my fingers. To my dismay, the chain snapped and fell out of my sight. But as I was about to give up, I noticed something floating away from the chain: a golden heart. A vision flickered in my mind of a similar locket I had once seen.

    My hand shot forward, and I grabbed the heart before it had a chance to swim away. Clasped between my fingers, I could feel the cold smooth metal, but I fought the urge to loosen my fist in order to look at it. I wasn't sure if it was fortunate or not, but as I was about to unfold my hand to take a peek, Salem appeared at the edge of the water. I quickly tucked the locket into the pocket of my hoodie and pretended that it wasn't there.

Unbelievable

Salem and I met my father and aunt outside of Jason and Mitchell's house. Paul had done his research ahead of time—Jason was working until 9:00 this evening at Howard's, and I knew Mitch was still working graveyard. We did a quick search around the backyard, but it was clear. There was no one around, human or vampire, besides the four of us.

"I am beginning to have my doubts of vampire activity," Salem commented as he watched Paul round the house another time, just in case.

"Do you still have a house key, Alex?" Paul asked, ignoring Salem completely.

"Yes. Why?" I asked, and then gasped. "Are you suggesting we break in?!"

"It wouldn't be breaking in. You own the house."

I shook my head. "No. There's no way. Besides, if a vampire was in there, there would be evidence—like a broken window or something, and Salem would be able to smell them."

Kim agreed with me, and Paul gave up on that idea. "Why don't you have a look around, kid?" he suggested to me. "You would know the place better than any of us."

"Okay." I sighed. Salem followed behind me, avoiding my father's glare. "I really doubt we're going to find anything."

But, unfortunately, I was wrong. My voice caught in my throat when I saw it, and Salem's eyes followed my gaze. Lying across the windowsill of what had once been my room was a strand of curly strawberry blonde hair.

"Oh, no," I groaned, feeling my legs wobble. "This has to be a coincid-" I stopped myself before I completed the sentence. *There are no coincidences*, I reminded myself. "M-Maybe Mitchell has a girlfriend, who has hair exactly like Claire's ... "

"Or a girlfriend who is exactly like Claire," Salem suggested, and I glared at him. "I'm sorry, Alex, but it is a possibility."

"Either that or she is a vampire, or some other form of supernatural monster!"

"What are you two fighting about back here?" Paul called as he and Kim approached us.

"We aren't fighting. Alexis just found a hair," Salem answered before I had the opportunity.

"That's a sign that someone has been here—vampire or otherwise," Kim said, examining the lock of hair from afar. "Recognize it, anyone?"

I kept my mouth shut. I wasn't going to drag them into this mess—for all I knew Salem was right, and Mitchell was dating Claire all of a sudden. Either that or she was a vampire, hunting me down and tracked my scent to this house. My stomach churned as I over-analyzed the situation.

Salem appeared to notice my discomfort and wrapped an arm around me. "Are you okay?" he whispered into my ear.

"I don't know ... let's go home," I mumbled.

"Do you feel well enough to drive?" His voice was full of concern.

"Is something wrong with her?" Paul's voice sounded irritable.

"She is just a bit woozy."

"Is she about to phase?" Kim asked in awe, knowing that was one of the signs. There was no doubt she was eager to see it again.

"No, she's not," Salem replied, holding me up completely as my legs gave out. "She is just really tired. She has been suffering from nightmares lately and hasn't slept much."

"Well, she shouldn't be driving. Let me take her home," Paul insisted.

"No!" I shouted, "No ... I'll be fine. I'm feeling better, really. You two can go."

Kim looked wary, but grabbed her brother's shoulder and led him away from us. "She'll be fine, Paul. She is probably just feeling uneasy about being here, considering the circumstances."

I watched my father and aunt walk out of the yard, across the sidewalk and into the Jeep Wrangler parked at the curb. Salem held me up until I felt stable enough to stand on my own. I hesitantly grabbed the hair and sniffed it, but I could smell nothing unusual.

"I know this is going to sound bizarre, but would you smell this for me?" I asked, offering the strand to Salem.

He didn't even question me before giving it a whiff. "Vanilla," he said, handing it back to me but my hands fell to my side. The strawberry blonde hair fell into the grass beneath us.

With a groan, I fell to my knees and held my head in my hands. "This can't be happening!"

"What is it?" Salem crouched beside me. "It has something to do with Claire, doesn't it?"

I barely nodded my head. "She smelled strongly of vanilla the day we met. What does this all mean?"

"I don't know, Alex," he answered and frowned. "Let's go home."

"How can I go home knowing she could be back at any moment?"

"And just what would you do if she showed up right now?"

"I don't know!" I said with an agitated tone. "There's just something going on, and I know it!"

"We'll ask Karen about it tomorrow, all right? Perhaps she will know something useful."

"Maybe..." I grumbled in agreement and retreated to the Alero.

When we returned home, I ate a quick dinner then ran upstairs to take a shower. As I removed my sweater I heard something clatter to the floor. The golden heart twirled around on the tile then came to a sudden stop as it hit the side of the bathroom cabinet. It fell open and I nearly screamed when I saw the picture inside. Lifting it carefully to get a better view, and to confirm that I wasn't imagining things, I closely admired the image held within the tiny gold heart.

On the left side was a black-and-white picture of a girl I recognized immediately. My hands trembled, causing me to nearly drop it. I forgot all about showering and ran downstairs, as steadily as I could. Salem was sitting in the nook chair reading when I came into the living room.

"Salem," I could barely speak, "you might want to look at this."

He put the book aside and took the locket from me. The grief in his eyes was unbearable. "Hannah ... " His voice was a mere whisper. "Where did you find this, Alex?"

"It was in the creek, stuck between some rocks," I explained. "I had forgotten about it until now."

"I don't understand ... " His eyes were focused on the picture; a mixture of pain and confusion swept across his face. "How could this be here?"

"I don't know." I frowned. "The only explanations I can think of are that Raziel had it while he was here, or Hannah has been here."

The confusion cleared. "That must be it. Raziel must have had it," he said with a sigh. "May I keep it?"

I almost laughed. "Of course." I embraced him tightly and felt his arms wind around my waist. "I wish it had just been an ordinary old locket."

"I don't," he replied, to my surprise. "It's amazing, really ... It belonged to Hannah, and I never imagined I would see or feel anything of hers ever again."

"Well, in that case, I'm glad I found it." I smiled up at him, and he kissed me lightly.

"As am I," he replied.

"I guess I should go to sleep," I said with a sigh. "Tomorrow will be here before I know it."

He agreed and placed the locket on the bookshelf then followed me upstairs.

Picnic

The sun was out once more, which made Salem slightly more hesitant to have a picnic because he feared Karen would be startled by his pale complexion. He was even more reluctant when I offered to cover him in foundation to make him appear tan. I stayed indoors to take the shower I skipped last night, while he went out to the lake and started setting up the picnic.

I quickly dressed in something simple—a dull gray tank top and denim shorts—and ran downstairs when I heard the doorbell ring. I was confused at first. It was the first time I had ever heard the melodic sound; no one had visited before. My mood shifted from excited to disappointment when I saw two silhouettes behind the doors. As I opened them, my heart sank. Standing beside my tall blonde friend was her shorter, younger cousin. With much effort, I forced a welcoming smile across my lips and invited them inside.

"Wow! This place is amazing!" Karen exclaimed as she eagerly entered the house. Her eyes were wide as she took everything in. "Found a rich one, huh, Alex?!"

I laughed and shook my head. "No. He's not rich."

"Right, whatever you say," she said and rolled her eyes. "People who aren't rich usually live in huge houses with tons of fancy stuff."

Claire seemed much less impressed. I wondered if she was somehow used to luxury. The only object in the room that seemed to catch her attention at all was the bookshelf. When she noticed my eyes were on her, she looked away and pretended to become fascinated by the white piano instead.

"So, where is this guy, anyway?" Karen asked after she finished absorbing her surroundings.

"He's out by the lake getting the picnic ready," I commented, still watching Claire. She was now standing beside Karen, focused on the back door. I was somewhat cautious about going out just yet, in case he wasn't done summoning everything. "He told me to wait here with you guys until he came back to let us know everything was ready," I lied.

At that very moment, my cell phone vibrated on the end table beside the sectional. Salem's name appeared across the screen.

"Everything ready?" I asked when I answered his call.

"The picnic is set and awaiting your arrival," he replied and hung up.

"Sounds like everything's set," I said with another false grin and led the girls through the back door.

"Wow, it's beautiful out here, too, Alex," Karen said as she admired the vast blue lake. Claire seemed moderately impressed by the views as we walked across the crisp green grass. Salem had his back to us, standing at the very edge of the water. His black hair shimmered elegantly as the sun hit it. My eyes settled on the thick blue blanket spread out across the ground. There was a stack of paper plates and plastic cups, and a pitcher of pink lemonade sat atop a round tray. In the center of the blanket were a basket and a bowl of grapes. I could distinctly smell fresh bread, which led me to believe we would be having sandwiches.

Karen's eyes were set upon the mysterious figure she had been dying to meet. I could feel my heart pounding within my chest, suddenly overcome with anxiety. What if it was obvious that he wasn't normal? Would they notice? I reminded myself that I hadn't noticed anything strange about him when we first met, but I also considered the fact that we weren't in bright daylight at the time. Salem was wearing a short-sleeved, silk blue V-neck shirt and black slacks; I wondered if the girls would find his attire awkward. I approached him quietly, took his hand and wheeled him around to face my friend and her cousin. Karen's eyes lit up as they did any time they fell upon a good-looking boy, whereas Claire didn't seem impressed—in fact, she looked more surprised by his appearance than anything else.

"Girls, this is Salem," I said with a grin.

"Wait!" Karen gasped. "I remember you!"

Salem smiled somewhat with recognition. "You directed me to Alex's car the day before her birthday."

"Well, you have apparently met Karen before." I laughed. How had I completely forgotten that fact? "And this is her cousin, Claire."

Claire's gaze fell on me when I spoke her name, then turned toward Salem. "Hello," she said in her magnificent voice.

"Hello," Salem repeated with a strange look in his eyes that I couldn't quite place. "Shall we?" he asked, gesturing toward the picnic.

I sat beside Salem on the left side of the blanket, while the two girls sat on the opposite end. Claire took no interest in the food, reminding me of how she had seemed to reject her drink in the cafe. Salem at least made an effort to pretend, pouring himself a cup of lemonade and sipping it every now and then. I poured myself and Karen a cup – it was the perfect combination of sweet and sour. There were four ham and cheddar sandwiches in the basket, I offered one to each of them. Salem neglected his, just as Claire ignored hers. I watched her closely as I bit into my sandwich, wondering just what would possess her not to eat. My mind wanted to wander into the darkest of thoughts, but I couldn't allow it right now—perhaps she had an eating disorder of some sort. She was awfully thin after all. I noticed Salem deliver me a simple wink as he popped a grape into his mouth, and I fought back a chuckle as I wondered what sort of effect ingesting real sustenance had on him.

"This is all wonderful!" Karen exclaimed, talking more so about the scenery than the food. "I can't believe you got so lucky, Alex."

"Uhh, thanks, I think." I laughed and returned to my sandwich.

"How long have you lived here?" Her voice was now directed toward Salem. Slight jealousy boiled in my blood as I watched the way she ogled at him.

"I have been here in Colorado for…a few years," he commented, smiling once at her before turning his gaze toward the lake. I knew he had been here far longer, but he couldn't quite tell them that he had been here for a period far longer than his apparent 'age'.

She thought for a moment, and then asked, "Where's your family?"

He cringed at the mention of his relatives. "They passed away, a little while after I moved here," He lied again.

"Oh, no!" Karen frowned. "I am so sorry to hear that!"

"It is tough, but I have managed without them." Salem shrugged, although I knew how terrible he felt. Claire appeared to glare in his direction for a mere moment—or perhaps I had imagined it.

"Do you play the piano?" Karen asked after finishing her sandwich, in an attempt to change the subject.

Salem smiled. "Not often. It was more of a gift for Alexis."

My eyes widened. "What? You never told me that!"

A light wisp of laughter escaped his smiling lips. "You never asked."

Then my stomach churned as the question came from Karen, "You play the piano, Alex?"

I coughed on the last bite of my sandwich. "Yeah. Sometimes..." My cheeks flushed vermilion as I tried to look away.

Salem put his hand to my chin and lifted my face to look at him. "It's nothing to be ashamed of." He looked now at Karen and said, "She plays very beautifully. I am surprised you didn't know."

I groaned and jabbed him in the shoulder with my elbow. "People from my school sort of make fun of the kids in music class, Salem."

"I had no idea." He frowned, "Regardless; it still isn't something you should be ashamed of. You should let them listen to your song."

I shook my head. "No, no ... They wouldn't want that."

"Oh, I'd love to hear it," Claire said with a bizarre smile.

"You would?"

"Of course. I'm very curious."

I sighed. "Fine. But, if Jason hears anything about it—you're both in big trouble! He'd never let me hear the end of it."

"I won't tell him, I swear."

Salem stayed outside to clean up while I led the girls back to the house. My fingers were shaking nervously as I edged toward the beautiful white piano that was *mine*. I could not fathom the fact that this had been created solely for me. Claire and Karen crowded around me as I sat on the bench and rested my unsteady hands against the smooth keys. I swallowed back my anxiety, shut my eyes and let my hands do their thing. It was the same light, melancholic tune I had played in music class the first day Salem and I met—the song that I had affectionately titled Nevermore after my love of *The Raven*.

The music stopped, and the room fell silent. I waited impatiently for the outburst of laughter I was expecting from Karen; however, when I glanced back at her, her mouth was gaping open with amazement. Claire's eyes were focused elsewhere.

"That was ... I don't even know how to put it into words, Alex," Karen babbled. I barely heard her as I stared suspiciously in her cousin's direction.

"Thanks," I mumbled. "Could I talk to you upstairs for just a minute? In private?"

"Yeah, sure," she replied. "Besides, I'd love to see the rest of the house! That okay with you, Claire?"

Claire turned toward us suddenly, as if she had been daydreaming before. "What? Oh. Yeah...sure. I'll just look around down here."

Suspicions

Karen was beyond enthusiastic about the bedroom. She blabbered on about the beautiful bed, the bizarre mirrored floor, the canopy, the bay window that gave a clear view of the surrounding nature. I sat on the edge of the soft mattress, twiddling my thumbs as I pondered how to ask her what was on my mind.

"Is something bothering you, Alex?" she finally asked after she took a quick glance at the bathroom.

"Sort of," I admitted. "It's about Claire."

"What about her?" She sat beside me; her expression grew serious. "You don't like her?"

"No, that's not it ... do you know if she is seeing Mitchell?"

Karen burst into laughter. "What?! No! She's never even met him or Jace. Why, do you have a thing for Mitch or something?"

"Funny." I looked at her sternly. "I just heard a rumor that some strawberry blonde girl has been hanging around at the house, and sneaking through Mitch's window. I just thought it might be her was all."

"Nah, it must be somebody else. She's not the only one with blonde hair you know." She smirked.

I nodded my head slowly, struggling to believe it. "That's all I wanted to ask you. I'm really glad you got to come over and meet Salem and everything."

"Me too. He's amazing, Alex. You are one lucky lady!" She giggled.

"Thanks, Karen." I laughed and hugged her briefly.

As we walked down the spiral staircase, I could hear Salem talking quietly to Claire. I could barely make out any of their words, but she seemed to be questioning him about the locket. So that is why her gaze kept lingering on the bookshelf—the locket. What was it about that heart that she was so interested in? They fell silent when we approached, and I saw Salem carefully tuck away the locket.

"It was a pleasure meeting you, ladies," he said when Karen approached her cousin's side, "however, I believe it is time you ought to go home."

"Oh, of course," Karen said politely. "Thank you so much for letting us come by! I hope we didn't overstay our welcome or anything."

"Not at all," Salem said with a polite smile.

"Yes ... " Claire said, "thank you for showing us your home." Something in her tone made me uncomfortable.

"Hopefully we can do it again sometime," I replied, mostly toward Karen.

Karen gently hugged me, and before I had the chance to step away, Claire laid a gentle hand upon my shoulder. The same jolting, electric feeling swam through my veins— and if I wasn't mistaken, Salem noticed it.

I watched quietly as the two girls walked through the tall white doors and vanished from sight. With a sigh of relief, I threw my arms around Salem and buried my head in his chest. His thin, cold arms crossed behind my back as he held me against him and rested his head on the top of mine.

"I wish you would have told me before that the piano was for me ... " I whispered.

I could feel his lips form a smile against my hair. "I apologize if I embarrassed you."

"You didn't. Karen actually liked my song," I said in awe.

"That doesn't surprise me. It is magnificent." His embrace tightened somewhat. "You are right about something being unusual about Claire."

"I know. And I found out, according to Karen, that Claire has supposedly never met Jason or Mitch, let alone been to the house."

"I observed some unusual behavior," he commented. "She appeared fascinated by Hannah's locket. She did not eat, nor drink, during the picnic. And as she was leaving, I believe she did ... something to you."

"It was that same feeling I mentioned the first time I saw her." I shuddered. "Do you think that's what caused the nightmares?"

"I hope not," he replied as he hugged me even tighter. "There was also something bizarre about the way she smelled."

"Vanilla?" I asked, staring up at him. "That's nothing unusual. Lots of girls smell that way."

He smiled and shook his head. "I must admit that I sometimes forget you cannot smell things quite as strongly as I can. I believe the excessive amount of vanilla perfume is being used to cover something up."

"Like what?"

"You may have been right to speculate that she might be a vampire," he replied scornfully. "And if that is the case, she has done her research and taken a lot of effort to attempt to cover it up."

"Why would she do that?"

"I do not know." He sighed. "Perhaps she is afraid someone will discover her secret."

"Well, she's doing an awfully good job of not looking like a vampire, if she is one. And it seems pretty strange that she would be around Karen all the time and willingly around me if she was, also," I said, trying to piece all the information together. "Unless she was trying to find me or something."

Salem tensed somewhat and released me from his embrace. "That is what I fear might be the case."

"You think she is? Should I tell Paul and Kim?" I asked as I watched Salem begin pacing, deep in thought.

"Not until we know for certain what we are up against. We don't want to have them hunting down a human, if somehow we are wrong."

"Do you think I should at least warn Karen?"

"If Claire wanted to hurt Karen, she would have done so by now," he replied. "I think you are her target, although I don't know why."

Warily, I curled up in Salem's bed that evening. My mind was overflowing with haunting thoughts that I only wished would go away. The feeling of Claire's touch made me even more hesitant to sleep, almost knowing that I was going to delve straight into the nightmares I had briefly escaped. Salem remained downstairs. The floorboards barely creaked under his weight as he paced back and forth. I could only imagine what was going through his mind.

My eyelids involuntarily fell shut as I listened to the rhythmic creaking sound. I fought off sleep for as long as I possibly could. The attempts at opening my eyes and staring out the window failed me repeatedly, each time I tried they would quickly fall shut once more. The exhaustion was suddenly overwhelming, and I could feel myself drifting away.

At first, everything was shrouded in mist. I could hear two distinct voices—Salem's and Claire's. Slowly, they came into view. They were outside of the house. Salem was at least ten feet away from her. Her expression was fierce and frightening as she approached him.

"What are you doing here, Claire?" he asked, not even the slightest hint of fear in his voice.

"I think I forgot to mention just how truly thankful I was for being allowed to see your house." A devilish smirk played across her lips. "You see, Salem, I've been trying to find you for months now, but the scent of that human covered you up all too well. I can smell her on you even now. Her stench has seeped deep into your pores Salem, how truly disgusting it is," she spat.

"Looking for me? I had assumed you were after Alex," he said plainly. "After all, you were present at her former house."

"No, no, dear Salem." She laughed darkly. "It has been you this entire time. Out of some dumb luck, your little human pet let me know she was the one you had been staying with. I thought you two may be living there. The place still smelt so strongly of her, but all I found were two little boys. It was so hard not to kill them."

His eyes narrowed. "What do you want of me?"

"Daniel had once said I might find you here. I must admit that I sure was surprised when I found you had a relationship with one of...*them*. I would have thought you were stronger than that—better than that." She stopped within two feet of him, her hands on her hips. "That sort of reminds me...I don't think I will be needing that *cousin* of mine anymore now that I know where you are. I doubt she will be missed anyway, not the brightest bulb after all. After a simple bump in while I was looking around the school I saw the faintest glimpse of you deep in her thoughts. You wouldn't believe how easy it was to convince her I was some long lost cousin who had shown up for her graduation. Just another perk of being a vampire."

Salem maintained calm, although a shimmer of shock lit up his eyes at the word 'vampire', listening to her story and watching her every move. "Daniel ... " he whispered, and then asked, "and you claim to have seen Karen's thoughts?"

"He taught me a lot of things, Salem. A touch is all it takes to see someone's thoughts, or put yours into their head." She grinned maliciously, tugging at the lustrous strawberry blonde hair on her head. The wig fell away, landing gently on the ground. Salem's mouth fell open in shock when the locks resembling spun gold were revealed.

"H-Hannah ... " he gasped, stepping backward.

Hannah's lips pulled up in a playful, yet disturbing smile. "So, you *do* remember me! Here I was beginning to worry you had forgotten all about your beloved family, seeing how you have managed without us, as you put it."

"I...I didn't mean it like that, Hannah," he uttered, still in shock.

"Of course you didn't, just as you meant nothing harmful by abandoning Arthur and mother, leaving them to die in that fire," she hissed. "Daniel promised you would be strong, promised you held so much potential, but all I've seen is a pathetic little gnat! Feasting off animal blood! How can you ignore the temptation of her scent, Salem? Does the blood throbbing through her veins at night not beckon you?"

She spat as the next words escaped her mouth, "How can you assist her in hunting our kind?"

"There are more ways of feeding than killing people!"

Hannah shook her head in disgust. "She is your enemy, Salem. Our enemy! And you *love* her!"

"I do," he said quietly, confidently. "Just as Raziel...Daniel...loved our mother."

She growled. "Daniel loved Margaret before he became a vampire. You fell in love with a human knowing what you both were!"

"I feel no remorse for how I feel," Salem replied, "but I do feel deeply regretful for having lost my family in that fire. I thought I had lost you forever, as well."

"You feel no remorse for it yet!" she said, inching closer to Salem. He stepped away again, his back now up against the wall of the house. "Will you just wait around until she finally finds it in her to kill you, like it is in her nature to do with our kind?"

"She has no intention of killing me, just as I have no intention of killing her, despite that being in my nature."

"Oh, but she will. Once I am done with her."

Salem's expression changed; he was furious. "What do you mean by that?"

"Her nightmares of you killing her, those have all been my doing." She smirked, as though pleased with herself. "I have been waiting idly by for her to finally snap so I could see you go at each other's throats!"

Now he was confused. "You want her to kill me?"

"Why not?!" She laughed. "After all, you did kill my father!"

Before Salem had the opportunity to react, Hannah was up against him—her hand coiled around his throat, thick nails digging into his skin. "When all of this is through," she spoke through gritted teeth, "I want my locket back."

Salem cringed in agony and barely managed to slam a fist into Hannah's side, but she hardly flinched. "Silly brother, you must know that human blood makes us stronger! You are weak and useless, Salem!"

"No ... " His voice was barely audible, "you are the weak one, a slave to your hunger."

"Slave?!" Hannah burst out into giddy laughter. "I am no slave, Salem. Slaves hate what they are made to do. I love it. The struggling. The screaming. Right down to the last breath of their pitiful little excuse for a life!"

"You have been corrupted, Hannah ... " His voice quivered.

"You are too soft, Salem. Humans are food, nothing more. Don't you remember our dear mother telling us not to play with our food?" Another burst of giggles flew from Hannah's mouth. "I'll tell you what, dear brother. Prove to me you can become what you truly are. Kill Alexis and empty her veins. I will forgive all that you have done, and we can be a happy little family again. What do you say?"

"What?! I would never-"

"Then you will die," she yelled, interrupting him. Salem's eyes flickered violet, but before he had the chance to summon whatever object he had in mind, Hannah slammed his body into the wall. "I used to idolize you, and now look at you! You are pathetic!"

The sound of Salem's agonizing screams woke me immediately.

Why weren't they stopping? Why could I still hear the sickening sound of his shrill yells? I jumped up from the bed, my eyes slowly adjusting to the darkness. My feet led me to the bay window, and my stomach churned at the sight. My body convulsed, my bones twisted and molded until they were smaller and smaller. Before I let my body get ahead of my mind, I hopped onto my nightstand and struggled to direct my cell phone to my contact list. After a moment, a list of names revealed themselves across the screen. I quickly selected Paul's name, and the phone dialed. It occurred to me that I wouldn't be able to talk, but I hoped the sound of Salem's scream might alarm him enough to come find out what was going on. Shards of glass cascaded through the whirl of feathers as the body of the raven burst through the window.

    My wings flapped quickly behind me as I flew toward the scene. Salem lay motionless on the grass, his shirt tattered and covered in his own blood; his face turned away to where I couldn't see it. Hannah hovered over him; her teeth bared and ready to strike. I wasn't that familiar with how vampires killed each other, but this reminded me entirely too much of how Salem killed Raziel. My beak fell open and the harmonious screech caused Hannah to falter, but she didn't cover her ears. She scanned the sky until she found me, hovering fifteen feet overhead.

    "Ah, Salem's little pet!" she cooed mockingly. "I was afraid you would be too lost in your nightmares to come out and play."

    Salem struggled on the ground, the sound undoubtedly bothering him. I shut my mouth, and the sound faded. Why wasn't she affected by it?

    "I am much stronger than him," she said with distaste, as though she could hear my thoughts, "even more so than father, much to his surprise." She spoke of him so fondly.

    I wouldn't let my eyes fall upon Salem again; I couldn't bear to see his condition. Hannah kicked him to the side, and I heard the faintest groan escape him, causing my stomach to churn once more. I had never felt such fury before as I did at that moment. My wings were flat against my body as I dove downward, ramming my beak into the flesh of her abdomen. She barely seemed affected, although I knew the hot venom had to be running through her veins now.

"What did you do?!" She suddenly shrieked with pain. "You're just a bird!"

I couldn't respond, but dove at her again, delivering peck after peck until she showed signs of weakness. Salem uttered something incomprehensible as I went in for the kill.

"No, Alex!" he yelled. I could hear the pain in his voice—it was more than just physical. "Please ... "

"Oh, how lovely!" Hannah laughed as I flew at full speed at her. "He doesn't want you to kill me!"

A blur of movement flashed before my eyes. Hannah's fist smashed into me as I turned to glance at Salem. The scenery twirled around me as I flew through the air. I came to a sudden halt, skidding across the ground. My body elongated and I was human again, writhing in pain against the cool blades of grass. Hannah was beside me in mere seconds; her head cocked to the side as she glanced down at me.

"Pitiful," she said, shaking her head. "What does he see in you?" She spat on me, then kicked hard into my left side. The unmistakable sound of bones crunching rang through my body, but this time it was not from transforming.

I coughed, blood spurting out of my mouth. "Salem ... "

"Salem can't save you now, *raven*," Hannah laughed. "He doesn't love you enough to save you—he'd rather see you die at my hands than lift a finger against me again."

"You're wrong!" I yelled, immediately regretting it as a burst of pain radiated through my broken ribs. As I writhed in pain, Hannah placed the bottom of her shoe into my neck. My thoughts were traveling into a darker place, a place where I knew this was the end, and I had no more chances left. As I lay there and braced myself for the inevitable breaking of my neck, a flicker of regret washed through my mind. Before I could reflect during my last moments of life, the sound of tires against gravel caught my attention. Was Paul here? Had he understood the urgency of the matter at hand?

Hannah perked her head up toward the sound, her eyes wild with curiosity. She lifted her foot and gave me a devilish smile. "Don't go anywhere, okay, sweetie? I'll be right back." Leaving my side, she ran to investigate what this noise was.

Within seconds I heard a terrifying shout of agony—it wasn't Paul's voice; it was Hannah's ...

"Alex?! Salem?!" Paul shouted anxiously, but he sounded so far away.

I heard movement nearby. Salem was on his feet. He must have healed enough to be mobile again. I felt his cold palm against my cheek.

"Don't leave me, Alex," he begged, cradling my head in his hands.

Options

    With wide eyes, I scoured the area. Paul was pinning Hannah against the wall, an arrow piercing her throat—the poison from it combined with my own must have finally been weakening her. The sun was breaking through gray clouds overhead, and I could feel something cool and sticky against my shoulders. After momentary confusion, I realized it was Salem's hands gripping me tightly and shaking me awake.

    "Alex?" he whispered soothingly, "can you hear me?" I could distinctly hear the worry in his voice.

    My head throbbed miserably as I nodded.

    He smiled faintly. "I am so glad you called Paul before coming out here."

    Another slow nod. "Why are your hands so sticky?" I managed to say.

    The faint smile was gone immediately, and he held his hands up to where I could see. Crimson stained his fingertips and palms. Was it my blood or his? Both? "You are bleeding ... a lot," he choked out, answering my unspoken question.

    I hadn't noticed the ache coursing through my body, the moisture that made my shirt cling to my abdomen and chest, nor the faint coppery smell that surrounded me. The panic came quick when I realized how much damage had been done. My lungs burned with each labored breath. I could barely remember any of what had happened.

"Am I going to die?" I asked in horror, tears beginning to fall down my cheeks.

Salem shook his head at me; the despair in his eyes was overwhelming. "I won't let that happen, Alex."

I attempted to smile at him. "It's not exactly something anyone has control over, S-Salem…" I coughed. The motion shot pain throughout my entire body.

"I might," he muttered quietly, "but hopefully it doesn't come to that."

"What's going to happen to Hannah?"

I watched his eyes lift upward, toward Paul and his half-sister. "I don't know," he replied, his expression uncertain. "She may be too corrupt to save … "

"Maybe … " My body convulsed painfully, and I clung tightly to Salem's arm, "M-maybe you can convince her … to see things your way."

He didn't seem concerned with her anymore, his focus fully on me now as he pulled me close. "That's not important right now. I need to ask Paul a question … but I don't want to leave your side."

I smiled weakly at him. "I'll be okay … "

"Don't leave me, Alex … " he repeated, kissed me gently on the forehead and lowered me onto the cool green grass. "I will be right back. Please hang on…for me."

My vision was blurred as I attempted to watch them. Hannah was still pinned up against the back wall of the Victorian, the venom weakening her to the point that she could barely move. It was amazing that she was so strong, even Raziel didn't possess her strength. There were at least ten slender arrows puncturing her skin in numerous places now. Paul held her firmly at the wrists, and I saw Salem approach him.

"How is she doing, Salem?" Paul asked, his voice trembling. He appeared to want to glance in my direction but fought the temptation.

Salem's back was to me now, trying to shelter me from their words, but I could still make them out, "Not good ... I don't know if she has much time left ... "

"I will kill you both if Alexis dies, you hear me?" Paul stated furiously. "I don't care who she used to be to you, or anyone."

"I understand," Salem whispered. "I need to ask something of you."

"What?"

"Before I say anything, promise you will listen before you react. This isn't something I want to do either, but I am afraid we have no other options."

Paul eyed him suspiciously. "What are you talking about?"

"What would happen to Alex ... " his words broke off, his voice unsteady, "if she had to be turned, if that was the only way to save her?"

The fury in my father's eyes was evident even through my foggy vision. My heart beat accelerated when I understood what Salem was asking him. "There has to be something else we can do," he replied through gritted teeth.

"I am afraid there may be no other way, Paul," Salem said regrettably. "I do not want this any more than you do."

Hannah hissed, "Do us all a favor and let her die!" She laughed wickedly until Paul elbowed her hard in the stomach.

"I'm not sure what would happen, Salem." Paul frowned, finally glancing at me. His eyes watered. "As far as I know, a Waldron has never been turned before. There's a chance that she might not be able to be. She already has the gift of turning into the raven, for all I know it could cancel each other out. Hell, the venom in her could hurt the vampire part, and she could suffer forever."

"Or she would only be capable of holding onto one ability. Or maybe she would carry both," Salem added thoughtfully.

"This is all wrong," Paul growled. "I was supposed to protect her from this! You were supposed to protect her!"

"There is no sense in dwelling on that right now. I fear we have precious little time to decide."

"This isn't a choice I can make," Paul said flatly, staring down at his feet. "I don't want to lose her, not like I lost Destiny ... but at the same time, I can't just let her become a monster."

"I won't let her become a monster," Salem vowed. "She can feed the way I do ... she doesn't have to be the enemy."

"If you are asking my permission, Salem ... I can't tell you yes or no. Just," I could hear my father's voice crack, "save her ... "

"Of course," Salem whispered, took one glance at Hannah, and retreated back toward me. My eyes were fearful when he approached me. "Don't be afraid, Alex, please ... "

"You said nothing was worth this!" I cried, "Not even you!"

"I was wrong," he said in a pained, hushed voice. "I can't let you die ... not like this. But I won't make the choice for you."

I wanted to laugh, but I fought it as hard as I could, knowing it would hurt. "So, this is what it takes to make you realize you want me to live? I had to be bleeding to death...for you to realize how fragile I am..."

He grimaced. "I was hopeful there would be another alternative, Alex. You must understand that I could never imagine life without you, but I could not bear to hurt you...to risk you becoming like Hannah." He shook his head in anguish. "Is this what you truly want? I need to know, now."

How was I supposed to decide this? What if my body rejected it, and I died despite his effort to save me? Would I be able to control myself and live like Salem, or would I become corrupted like Hannah? What about Jason, Mitchell, and Karen ... would I ever see them again, or would I be sacrificing that forever because I couldn't control my thirst? I had little other option right now—it was either this or die, but which was the lesser of the two evils?

I could already feel my life diminishing despite my attempt to hold on. Salem was right; there wasn't much time.

"Yes," I whispered with what might be my final mortal breath. It felt like such a simple answer, for such a huge decision.

Salem nodded solemnly, lifting my head in his hands and pressing his cold lips to my own. "I love you, Alexis," he said in a strained voice, "no matter what happens."

All I could manage was an obscure smile as he rested my head back on the moist ground—moist with my blood. I was barely holding on now, scarcely aware of my surroundings. Everything was fading before me. They say you see a white light when you die, but all I could see was darkness. As Salem's face grew dimmer and dimmer, I could hear the dull shout of his pleading voice, asking me to hold on just a moment longer ...

As I drifted, my mind began to wonder if I had made the right decision. Salem had once told me that when he became a vampire, his memories of being human were vague ... would I, too, be stripped of my memories? Would I forget who I had been?

Would I forget Salem? As I thought his name, I could feel his cold lips against my wrist. What if he couldn't control himself, what if the taste of my blood was too much? I felt something stab into me as he warily pierced the skin on my arm.

What if I didn't survive? I heard myself scream as his fangs sunk deep into my vein. I felt the warm blood flowing up through my skin. Then, I felt nothing.

Clouded

Feeling returned. It was dull, numb and far way. There was a mild burning in my arm; my mind couldn't focus on anything but that. I could not see—my eyes may not even have been open. There were no sounds, just the slight discomfort.

The silence was broken immediately when I heard the distant screaming. No. It wasn't distant at all. It was coming from me. The burning evolved into a piercing, unbearable pain all throughout my body. I could barely feel myself jerking around as I tried to escape whatever was hurting me. Something strong and cold held me still. A soothing voice promised everything would be okay. Was it the voice of the creature that was hurting me? No. Something so sweet, so sincere couldn't possess this power.

The burning returned, only this time it was more than a slight irritation in my arm. It felt as though the blood in my veins had been drained, replaced with battery acid. I twisted and contorted, fighting against my own molten core. Every inch of my skin felt as though needles were being dug into my body. The more I fought to get away from the pain, the harder I was held down.

I fought against the cold weight, fought to squirm and wriggle in agony as the pain intensified. I heard another voice—thick, masculine, afraid—begging that it be over quick. Then, a vile laughter caught my attention; it was endless. This must have been the sound of the monster upon me. That was the only explanation.

The darkness slowly faded. I could see a dim light above. The voices grew louder, closer. The pain was still there, but my body had become numb to it. The monster was still pinning me down, and I knew it was the cause of my pain. Fighting for my own survival, I screamed and kicked at it.

"It will pass quicker if you don't fight it, Alex," the soothing voice came again. It was close to me, so close I could smell it. It smelled fresh, sweet … like water, chamomile, something else I couldn't quite place. It reminded me somewhat of the smell of old books.

My surroundings became clearer. The dim light was now a bright radiant orb in the deep-blue sky; however, it did not hurt my eyes to stare into its intense, resplendent glow. There was a face near me; it seemed familiar, yet peculiar at the same time. The crimson of his eyes caught my attention instantly.

"How do you feel?" The consoling voice asked again. This could not have been the creature whose laugh had taunted my agony.

I blinked. How did I feel? Lost. Confused. Uncertain. Terrified. Pain incarnate. I could have come up with a list of thousands of words to describe the way I felt, but I couldn't find my voice. I turned my head away from the crimson-eyed figure, spotting two more bodies. One of them was slumped over against a wall, the other standing guard beside it as if waiting for it to attack at any moment.

With a gasp, my memories came flooding into my head. Janet. Desmond. Mark. Salem. Paul. Jason. Karen. Claire—no, Hannah. Last, but not least, I remembered who I was. The simple, brunette-haired girl from Willowshire, Colorado who less than a year prior discovered she wasn't at all who she thought she was. A vampire hunter, who fell in love with a vampire.

"Salem ... " I whispered, my eyes falling back on the familiar yet peculiar young man beside me. His face lit up when I spoke his name. The crimson eyes were still there—brighter than I had ever seen them before.

"How do you feel?" he repeated, running a hand across my forehead.

"Cold," I replied in a hoarse voice, my body shivering as I spoke. Of all the adjectives, that one best described how I felt. The hot, agonizing burn was now a vague feeling. I felt as though I was lying in a tub of ice. My body shook once more. "Why is it so cold?" I asked, staring back up at the sun.

"You will get used to it ... " he muttered quietly. "What do you remember?"

"Everything," I responded, peering downward at my body. My instincts told me to scream, but I somehow remained calm as I stared at the mess. Two ribs protruded from my side; a large gash tore across my abdomen, and blood was pouring from two small dots on my wrist. I watched in amazement as the wounds slowly closed, the ribs gradually fell back into place. "Shouldn't I be ravenously hungry...or something?" I asked as I sat upright.

Salem helped me sit, although I felt perfectly strong enough to manage on my own. "No, why? Are you?" He sounded mildly concerned.

I shook my head. "No, that's just what I was expecting."

His lips curved into a gentle smile. "Can you stand yet?"

"I think so," I replied and let him help me to my feet. I didn't feel even the slightest bit wobbly or weak.

"I want to test something. Try not to be alarmed." He spoke calmly. I watched his eyes twinkle violet, and a small knife appeared in his left hand.

"What are you going to do with that?!"

"You said that my suffering triggers your ability to phase," he replied, and to my horror, he drove the knife into his stomach before I had the chance to stop him. I stared in disbelief at him, but the familiar feeling of changing didn't occur. He groaned and tugged the knife from his flesh. "Why aren't you changing, Alex?" he asked through clenched teeth.

"I-I don't know," I stuttered. "Maybe I can't anymore."

"Focus," he whispered, tossing the knife aside. "Imagine yourself as the raven flying over the lake and back to me. Please."

Why was he so desperate for me to alter my appearance? Perhaps he was afraid he had taken not only my life, but my purpose away from me. I shut my eyes tightly and envisioned a raven ascending through the air, its vibrant wings glistening against the sunlight as they guided the bird across the majestic body of water. It took only a moment for me to realize my eyes were no longer shut and the fowl I saw was my reflection across the water's surface.

Salem stared in awe, and I noticed that Paul had taken his eyes off of Hannah to glance at me as well. I did an impressive flip and escalated higher into the air before diving down and landing gently on Salem's shoulder. I nuzzled my small head against his black hair, and he reached a hand up to caress my soft feathers.

"I was so afraid that I had stolen this from you," he said quietly. "Something does worry me, however."

"What?" I nearly fell off of his shoulder at the sound of my voice. I can't speak in raven-form! Perhaps I was only hearing my voice inside my mind. That was the only logical explanation ... but the expression on his face made me doubtful.

"Well, first of all—that was unexpected," he whispered as he stared at me with shocked, troubled eyes. "I don't believe I even saw your beak move ... "

"So ... you can hear me?" I blinked my beady black eyes at him, crooking my head sideways.

"Quite clearly," he replied. "What concerns me, though, is you shouldn't be so focused, so capable. Newborn vampires are practically drones to begin with; I believe that might be what affects our human memories. Yet you seem to have forgotten nothing, and you are showing signs of powers you didn't previously possess ... "

"Does that scare you?"

"No." He gave me a half-smile. "Not entirely, at least."

My gaze tore away from Salem's expression and trailed across the field of grass until they met Paul's. He looked not only distraught, but exhausted. Hannah, now seemingly unconscious, stirred slightly at his feet. My wings spread out at my sides, and I pulled away from Salem's shoulder and glided over to my father. With one swift, painless movement, I felt my body alter into its regular form.

"You should go home, dad," I said calmly as I placed a hand on his arm, "or at least go inside and lie down. You look like you're about to pass out."

Before I had any opportunity to react, Paul threw his thick arms around me in a tight hug. I could smell the salt of his tears as they fell upon my shoulder. I hugged him back, with one eye locked on Hannah. "I was so afraid I had lost you, Alex," he bawled. It was strange seeing him like this, especially given his usual tough demeanor.

"Well ... I'm okay, dad," I replied awkwardly, letting him relieve himself of the pain and suffering he had to endure. I couldn't imagine what it must have been like for him, watching his daughter come so close to death and then witness me becoming one of his enemies. "I'm okay now, really. Go get some rest."

Paul released me slowly, wiped at his strained eyes and nodded. I directed him to the back door and watched him stumble up the stairs and into the house.

Hannah

Once Paul was completely out of sight, I approached Hannah's slouched body. Delicately, I plucked each slender arrow from her skin; she flinched at each removal. Her eyes were beginning to open again, and I could tell that she was shocked to see me. Part of me knew I should be afraid, but I didn't feel even an ounce of fear.

"I'm surprised the venom didn't kill you," I commented as she lifted her head up to face mine. Her scent was stronger than ever before—hidden beneath the luscious vanilla was something foul. Salem had smelled so sweet in comparison, while her aroma reminded me of metal and burning wood. She looked bewildered, and I smirked. "This isn't turning out at all how you had planned, is it?"

Her head shook. "You're supposed to be dead! I killed you!" she barked.

"Salem saved me."

"So, the hunter has become the hunted!" She laughed coldly.

"Now, we have to figure out what to do with you," I snarled, fighting the urge to tear her apart. "The only reason you're not dead right now is because of your brother. I would kill you where you lie if it wasn't for him."

"What, you think I'm afraid of you?"

"You should be," Salem said, approaching us quietly and crouching down beside me. "Hannah ... I will never find it in me to forgive you for what you have done, but I will give you a second chance. Try to see my side of things, please."

"You are such an insignificant coward, Salem. What part of 'I enjoy this' did you not understand the first time?"

"Who is to say you wouldn't enjoy living like I do?" he said flatly. "Think back to before any of this happened. Remember mom, Arthur, Daniel," he spoke Raziel's true name with contempt, "remember how happy things were then ... "

I noticed a slight change in her expression—fondness. "Those times are gone, Salem."

"Yes, they are," he replied sadly. "However, there are families all around us that still have that. They still have each other; they still have the joy of life." His voice was light and gentle. "Think back to when that was taken from us, from you. Daniel may have elongated your time on earth, but look at everything he took away from you. Who are we to feed on these humans, to take away their lifetime of family and precious moments?"

"You did the same to your little raven," she interjected. "You took everything she could ever have in life from her!"

"That's where you are mistaken, Hannah," I said. "He gave me everything I could ever want in life. Had he not done this, I would be dead."

"Why would you of all people want this existence? You are a killer of our kind. Why would you even allow him to make you into that which you hate?"

"I don't hate your kind, only the ones who kill people. Not all of your kind is evil, Hannah," I replied. "Salem has shown me without a doubt that there can be good, even in a vampire. As far as wanting to be like this, well...for the longest time I was haunted by the idea of growing old while Salem ceased to age, ceased to change. I nearly begged him to change me, but he told me nothing was worth such a life—including him."

"What changed his mind?" She stared at me awkwardly.

"The fact that you nearly killed her!" Salem seethed with anger. "I couldn't bear to live without her, Hannah. I believe if Daniel had been given the chance, he would have done the same for mom ... "

"But instead, he picked you, Hannah," I said as the realization came over me. "He couldn't bear to be without you. He loved you."

"The only downfall of that is he let you become corrupted by his ways," Salem said with a frown. "If I had known you were still alive ... I spent years believing you were dead, when in fact I could have helped you long ago."

Hannah appeared distracted, barely listening to what her half-brother was saying. She sniffed the air, and then lunged at me without warning. I pushed her back with a strength I hadn't previously possessed. My hands gripped tightly around her wrists as she fought to reach my throat.

"She isn't one of us, Salem!" she wailed. "Don't you smell it? Can't you hear it?"

As her words sunk in I nearly lost my grip on her. I tuned out all other noises but the rhythmic yet faint thumping within my chest. "Salem?" I eyed him pleadingly for an answer. He looked just as befuddled as I felt. "What does this mean? How is this possible?"

Hannah relaxed somewhat, and I released her. She eyed me closely, suspiciously. "Something in her blood is stopping her from completely turning."

"Does this mean I am going to die, or that I'm not a vampire, or ... " I began rambling, my mind full of questions and concerns.

"I don't know what it means, Alex," Salem said quietly. "All I know is you're alive, and for now that is all that matters."

I couldn't agree to that. My questions needed answers, but I knew of no one that could help me. Even Paul, who knew so much about vampire and hunter history, had no idea because something like this was unheard of.

"Father would have known," Hannah commented coldly. "It's such a shame that you killed him!"

"You would have done the same thing had you been in my position," Salem argued harshly. "Now, are you going to take me up on my offer or am I going to have to kill you, too?"

Hannah's topaz eyes lingered on her half-brother's face for a moment. "I'm not making you any promises," she replied.

"You don't have to. Just try it, and if you don't like it ... " he paused, regret in his eyes, "we will let you go."

"Right, you will just let me go?" She laughed. "I don't believe that for a second."

"I promise, Hannah. What other choice do you have? Would you truly rather die than have to live off of animals?"

"Maybe," she glowered.

Salem rolled his eyes, which I noticed had finally returned to their natural pale blue. "Try it, Hannah. You might find that you enjoy it, after all."

"Fine," she replied bitterly.

"Good. Now, let us go inside, and you can tell me all about your abilities."

I was shocked that he had found it so easy to forgive Hannah, so easy to give her that second chance. Had it been my sister, would I have done the same thing? I really wasn't sure. There were other, more important things on my mind as I followed slowly behind Salem and Hannah into the Victorian. As much faith as I had in Salem, I didn't trust her, and wasn't sure I ever could.

When we walked inside, Paul was strewn across the sectional, snoring loudly. We passed by him and entered the kitchen. I watched Hannah warily, noting her every move. She appeared surprisingly uninterested in the scent of Paul's blood—I wondered how long that would last.

Recollections

Sitting across from Hannah at the dining table was awkward, not only because she was a blood-thirsty vampire but also because I had witnessed moments from her past, and I felt almost as if I knew her. Not to mention the fact that she almot killed me mere hours earlier. Salem sat beside me, his hand resting on my own. We were both tense, carefully observing the golden-haired girl.

"What do you want to know?" she asked, tapping her long silver nails against the table surface. I noticed the distinct British accent in her voice arising as she spoke, now that her true identity had been revealed. It caused me to wonder how long it took her to teach herself to speak without it.

"Everything," Salem said somewhat enthusiastically, "from the moment Raz ... *Daniel* ... took you from the house."

"I haven't thought of any of this in a lifetime...brace yourselves for a long story." Hannah smirked. It was relieving to see her in a calm, friendly mood, but I was still cautious, worrying that at any moment she could strike. "I can vaguely remember the fire. You were sleeping in my bedroom that night because I had a nightmare. Something woke me, and Daniel was standing in my room. Before I knew what was happening, he stole me away from the house. As I looked back I could see the smoke, and the red glow. I was horrified, but he assured me that everything would be okay—that you would be okay.

"He took me to a small house far away—he was unbelievably fast! After tucking me away safely inside and insisting that I stay put, he said he would save you, too. I never saw you, but he swore you were safe. He told me that Arthur and Margaret perished in the fire, and he held me as I cried myself to sleep.

"The following morning, he told me that he would protect me, no matter what. He said it wasn't going to be easy for him, that part of him wanted to hurt me more than I could even imagine. What way is that to speak to a child? I was frightened, of course, but I stayed with him. What choice did I have, being only three at the time? He stayed with me as often as he could, leaving when I was asleep or otherwise occupied with toys.

"Years had passed, and eventually I could fend for myself. Daniel would leave for hours, sometimes days, at a time—but he never failed to come back. I didn't see or speak to another person during the thirteen years he kept me there, but he took care of me. He treated me like the daughter he viewed me as. It wasn't until my sixteenth birthday that he finally told me who he really was," she paused, appearing deep in thought, "he told me what happened between him and Mother, and how she refused to tell me that he was my true father. Instead, she made me believe I was imagining him. I will admit that for a long time I hated her for keeping the secret from me.

"He told me what he was, what he did, and how hard it was for him to be around me. He told me how delicious I smelled to him, how tempted he was to kill me every time he was near. It was my choice, I told him to turn me into a vampire so that we could be together forever, so that he would not have that temptation." She smiled fondly at the memory. "Daniel was hesitant, much like Salem was about turning you, Alexis, but with time he agreed. After the process was over, he taught me the ways of being a vampire. I enjoyed every moment of the experience. We hunted together, and he was impressed by my strength and speed—more than even he was capable of. Then, he spoke of you ... Salem."

"I was long gone by then," Salem said quietly.

"Yes," Hannah agreed, "he told me how he kept you with him for a short period, hoping you would take to being a vampire as I had. You disgusted him, Salem. He expected so much of you ... you were his first. He told me that you decided to kill yourself rather than 'commit to a lifestyle of murdering humans'—those were your exact words, he said. You were convinced that daylight would end it all, but it was only a story he had told you to keep you from leaving, while he worked on molding you to be like him." Her voice grew slightly less affectionate. "You never returned."

I watched Salem nod his head. "If only I had known you were still alive then; you could have been mere miles away, and I never knew ... "

"It doesn't matter," Hannah said.

"And these abilities of yours?" he asked. "When did you discover those? What all are you capable of?"

She grinned. "I told you that my father taught me many things. He had a gift to see into the mind of whomever he touched, or put his thoughts into theirs. With time, I was able to take it beyond this. For the most part, everything I can do relates to the mind. I can manipulate dreams, as you should have gathered by now. The effect is only temporary, sadly, and requires contact between myself and the ... victim. Occasionally, I can see into people's minds without even needing a touch ... I haven't quite gotten the hang of that one yet, though. It worked on raven-girl's little friend Karen; that's how I knew about your *relationship*." She spoke the last word with strong distaste. "Daniel told me you had relocated to Colorado in search of some girl he foresaw in your future ... that's what brought us here. We had been traveling together."

"Did you get separated?" I asked.

"He told me to stay behind one night, that he had something private to take care of," she growled. "I followed his scent later that night, only to discover his remains in an unmarked grave."

"I will not apologize for what I did," Salem said, averting his eyes from her.

"Neither will I for what I did to your little birdy there."

"Right," he grumbled through gritted teeth.

"How did you manage to convince Karen you were her cousin?" I asked out of nowhere, partly to try to ease the tension.

"That was easy," she said with her melodic laugh. "She is far too gullible for her own good. It was hardly necessary for me to manipulate her with vampiric abilities; she easily went along with my story. I discovered her outside of the school and saw you in her thoughts, so I ran up to her and introduced myself as Claire Davidson and stated I had just transferred from a school in Wyoming because my parents found jobs here, and we had relatives in the area. I said I was looking for my cousin Karen Williams, and that I heard a rumor that she was a senior this year, about to graduate. She was so excited."

"How did you know she was one of my friends, how did you even know her name?" I asked suspiciously.

"As I said, I could see inside her mind," she explained. "If I have long enough to dig deep, I can see things that they are not even currently thinking about. Memories. Truths. I have to say, she was really easy to dig into, but anyway…that's how I learned her name, and of you."

"And you fooled Karen and me into thinking you were an average teenager by wearing makeup and heavy perfume?"

"Yep," she said and smirked. "I should have known my dear brother here wouldn't have been as easily tricked."

As we were in the middle of our discussion, I heard a loud bang in the other room. I turned and saw that Paul had rolled off of the sectional. With a grunt, he clambered back onto it in a sitting position and glanced groggily in our direction. Within seconds, he was on his feet, crossbow in hand aimed directly at Hannah.

Needs

The arrow whistled through the air. Hannah ducked down under the table, and I watched as the arrow sped through the kitchen before impaling one of the mahogany cabinets. Salem shot an angry glare at my father and within seconds was beside him, ripping the weapon from his grasp.

"Have you lost your mind?!" Paul roared, trying to push Salem away. "That monster almost killed Alex, and you just let her in here?!"

"Relax, dad," I said from the dining room. "We're trying to come to some sort of agreement. She can't help what she is, just like I can't help what I am."

Paul shook his head in disgust. "I won't allow this, Alex. You're a hunter; you don't protect them!"

"You've been *letting* Salem and I protect each other for months. This isn't any different," I glowered.

"I should just kill all of you now and end this!" he replied, to my surprise. "You're one of them now … "

"No, not exactly," Salem uttered from beside Paul.

"What do you mean by that?"

"She isn't a vampire, Paul ... at least, not entirely. She still has a heartbeat."

Paul looked suddenly alarmed. "That's not possible."

"Apparently, it is," Salem replied. "But, we are not sure what it means. We were actually hoping you had some input."

My father shook his head. "A Waldron has never been changed before, like I said earlier ... I don't know what it could mean," he paused, rubbing his forehead as he thought, "there might be one person who has an answer for us, but I haven't talked to him in years."

My eyes perked up when I heard there might be someone who could help solve this mystery. "Who?" I asked with growing curiosity.

"It won't be easy to get to him, especially in private," he said and sighed. "Your grandfather."

My grandfather? I hadn't even considered the idea that I had a grandparent who was alive. How had I not asked about them before? Probably because I was so caught up in other things, plus it wasn't like Paul ever made the effort to mention them.

"Where is he now?" I asked, my mind still wandering with ideas and speculations on just who my grandfather was, what he was like, and why I had never heard of him.

Paul grimaced and sat back on the sectional. "Your grandfather is locked up in a mental institute."

"What?!" My eyes widened in shock. "Why?"

"It's a long story, kid," he grumbled. "He was a great hunter during his youth, but once your grandmother passed away about five years ago, things got out of hand. I'm not sure if it was the loss of her, or something else—but he just wasn't himself. He would publicly speak of vampires, of hunting, warning random people to be on the lookout for monsters ... " He stretched across the couch once more. "Eventually he was reported for supposedly attacking some innocent woman, claiming that she was a vampire. That didn't go over too well as you can imagine."

"Wow ... " I said quietly, my mouth wide in shock. "When was the last time you talked to him?"

Now my father looked ashamed. "I've not seen him since he was admitted."

"What?! Why not?" I gasped. "That's horrible."

"You wouldn't understand, Alex," he said glumly. "He's just not the same man anymore. I doubt he'd even recognize me now."

"That's not the point. I would visit you even if you supposedly went crazy, especially when I understand that some of those things *are* real."

"Maybe you're right," he replied guiltily. "Not to change the subject, but I'm starvin'. You think there's any way that I could, well you know," he nodded towards Salem, "get something to eat?"

"Now that you mention it, I'm kind of hungry, too ... " I said.

Salem eyed me curiously, and then turned to glance at Paul. "What do you want?"

"Roast," he mumbled in response. "Destiny always made a real good pot roast."

I was taken aback somewhat at the mention of my birth mother's name. There was very little I knew about her, but I was afraid to ask—especially now. I observed the brief glow in Salem's eyes and watched a steaming bowl of broth, carrots, meat, potatoes, and onions appear on the coffee table before my father. Before I had the opportunity to request a meal of my own, Salem was at my side, dragging me away from my seat and leading me to the front porch.

"What is it?" I asked as he released my wrist.

"You said you were hungry," he replied quietly. "Do you think ... " he hesitated, "are you hungry for food or blood?"

My eyes grew as I registered what he was asking. "I-I don't know. How would I know the difference?"

"Do you have any cravings for real food?"

"No, not specifically, anyway." I replied. "But does that really mean I need blood?"

"I don't know what you need anymore, Alex," he replied sadly. "But, there's only one way to find out."

"Are you trying to tell me I need to go kill a squirrel or something?" I asked in disgust.

"Maybe. We have to figure out just what your body needs."

"Well, I can tell you right now, my mind says my body doesn't want that!" I shuddered at the mere thought.

Salem smiled gently. "Regardless, we need to find out. It won't hurt to try, and it might satisfy that hunger."

"Fine," I drawled.

It wouldn't have mattered nearly as much if my transformation had been complete—then I am sure I would have been all for it. In fact, I probably would have tackled Paul the second I saw him. While I was fortunate that I hadn't, I did wish I actually felt eager to do this ... it would make it a lot easier. I felt sick to my stomach merely thinking about what Salem was about to have me do.

I followed him toward the clearing, running faster than I was ever capable of before. The trees, boulders, and berry-speckled bushes all flew passed me as we stormed through the forest. It wasn't quite as amazing as flying because everything went by in a flash, but it was still exhilarating. Within mere moments we were at the edge of the creek. I stared into the crystal-clear water, spotting the exact location I had discovered Hannah's locket. Suddenly, I felt very alert. My eyes darted toward something rustling among the bushes ten feet ahead. I could smell the coppery sweet scent of blood. I stood still, sniffing the air for a moment longer. Another scent had caught my attention—wet fur. I could hear the distinct sound of a tiny heart beating. While it made me sick, it also excited me. Salem appeared to notice my reaction; undoubtedly, he sensed the creature too by now.

"At least some part of you wants it," he said. I wasn't sure, but he almost sounded disappointed.

I was disappointed. Without thinking, I sped toward the distant bush. My eyes were wildly scanning the area, my ears listening for even the tiniest sound. The animal barely had the opportunity to run before I had my hands around its wriggling, wet body. I gasped and nearly dropped it when I stared at the panicking little butterscotch rabbit. How could I possibly hurt this adorable creature? I looked pleadingly at Salem.

"You've already scared it, Alex," he said calmly, a few feet behind me. "Rabbits are known to die of heart attacks when incredibly frightened. You might as well put it out of its misery while you still can."

I gulped, staring at the beady little eyes looking back at me. Then, as I felt its heart beating against the palms of my hands I felt a sudden desire to rip the creature to pieces. Slowly, I felt a pinch of unfamiliar pain in the front of my mouth. *Fangs*, I thought in horror.

My lips were against the rabbit's fur at once, my fangs digging deep into its skin and tearing at it. I didn't think. I didn't feel. I just let the warmth of the blood run down my throat. Soon the hunger was gone; the need had vanished, but something didn't feel right. The guilt was overwhelming. My grip loosened, and the lifeless rodent plummeted toward the ground.

    I ran to Salem, tears streaming down my cheeks as I hid my face in his shirt—no doubt staining it with the moist blood from around my mouth and hands. He held me quietly, letting me release the anguish I felt. I wondered if he had felt the same the first time he committed such an act. I tugged away from him and started running toward the creek.

    "Alex?" He stared after me, then followed behind.

    I knelt at the water's edge and stared in awe and horror at my reflection. My skin was paler, but it was nothing compared to the snow-white complexion of Salem or Hannah. There was a hint of rosy warmth in my cheeks still, but the thing that caught my attention the most was the ring of red around my otherwise hazel eyes. My hands plummeted into the water, rinsing away the evidence of what I had done and scattering my horrible reflection. I watched the swirl of red dye the once clear liquid, then brought a handful up to my face and wiped it clean. If only I could wipe away the red in my eyes ...

    Was this truly what I had wanted? I felt Salem kneel beside me and pull me away from the creek. He laid me against the dew-covered grass and held me against him. His body felt cold, but not nearly as much as before.

    "I'm sorry," he whispered lightly into my ear. His cool breath tickled the nape of my neck.

    "For what?" I asked, staring up into the sun and resting my hand across his abdomen. He tightly gripped my hand with his own.

    "For doing this to you."

"It was my choice, remember? It is what I wanted," I replied quietly.

He lifted his head up to look at me, grief displayed across his flawless face. "What if it isn't, Alex? What if there is still the possibility that you will age and die as you previously feared, because you are in fact not a full vampire? For all we know you could still only have one life to live, but have to suffer through it as..."

My mouth opened to speak, but no words came out. I hadn't considered that fact. "I-I don't know ... "

"Exactly." He frowned.

"Well, no sense in worrying about it until we find my grandpa," I replied. "And if that proves to be useless, we'll just have to find someone else that knows."

Salem didn't reply. He simply lay down beside me, breathing ever-so-gently, and I felt another unexpected feeling overcome me—sleepiness. With a stifled yawn, I curled up beside him and let myself drift away to sleep as I watched the sun fading in the darkening sky.

The Locket

How much time had passed was a mystery to me when I felt Salem shake me awake. I blinked my eyes open and stared in disbelief. We were laying upstairs in his bedroom in complete darkness. The black curtains were drawn closed, and there wasn't even a hint of sunlight through the thin material.

"Was it all a dream?" I asked quietly, rubbing my eyes and stretching.

"No," he replied flatly. "Paul and I are both worried about you, Alex."

My eyes blinked again and settled on his. "What? Why?"

"You shouldn't need to sleep."

"It's not like sleep is a bad thing, though. So what if I am still mostly normal?"

"You have been sleeping for over a day, Alex."

"What! No ... There is no way."

"I have attempted to wake you numerous times," he stated. "Paul almost forced me to rush you to a hospital because he thought you were in some sort of coma."

I groaned and covered my head with a pillow to mask the intensity of my scream. Salem plucked the pillow away and stared at me. "Was that really necessary?"

"I think so," I replied hoarsely, my throat now sore. "What all have I managed to hibernate through, anyway?"

"Not a lot. Paul has been frantically worried this whole time. Hannah has behaved well, much to my surprise. I half-expected her to have killed him by the time I brought you back here. I cannot believe it slipped my mind not to leave them alone together while we went off to hunt."

"Oh … " I gasped. "I hadn't thought of it either. I was so hungry…then so tired."

He smiled faintly. "I do feel kind of useless now."

"What are you talking about?" I asked, sitting up on the bed and staring at him.

"I am so used to serving you breakfast every morning."

"Well, summon me a rabbit." I laughed half-heartedly. This did have me wondering though. "Why don't you ever summon your 'food' instead of risking getting spotted out hunting animals with your bare hands?"

"There are limitations on my ability," he replied glumly. "I can't summon anything that is living."

"Ah, I see. Can you do me a favor?"

"Anything."

"Summon me something simple. Like a chocolate-chip cookie or something."

He looked at me awkwardly, then with a flicker of his eyes, a cookie appeared on his held out palm. "Here…"

"Thanks," I said with a smile. "So how do you feel when you eat regular food? Like, the grape you had during the picnic."

"Sick," he replied.

"Food doesn't taste good to you at all?"

"No."

As I contemplated this, I bit into the soft texture of the cookie. It tasted sweet and delicious and had me longing for more. "So I shouldn't be enjoying this so much, then?"

He sat up and gave me another awkward stare. "You are enjoying it?"

"Oh, yeah! It's delicious," I replied, biting into it again.

"Bizarre," he said quietly, watching me intently.

"Why couldn't we have tried this first, you know...before tormenting the poor little bunny?" I asked as I popped in a piece of cookie I had ripped off.

"I don't know ... I had just assumed you would be like me," he replied.

The tone in his voice made me sick to my stomach. He sounded hurt and confused—no doubt still concerned with what he had done to me. For the time being, I had decided I wasn't going to let it bother me. I would find my grandfather, regardless how difficult it ended up being, and get answers from him. Until then, I would take things as they came, and enjoy the benefits of both worlds.

Paul nearly tackled me when I finally arrived downstairs, engaging me in another tight unbreakable hug. I laughed nervously when he released me, noting his appearance. He looked like he hadn't slept in hours. "You look terrible." I frowned.

"Wow, thanks. You would too if..." He sighed. "I'll get a nap in here soon. I should probably check in at the shop. I bet Kate's going crazy over there. I gave her a few calls but, well, you kind of know her."

"Yeah, I can imagine," I replied. "Get some sleep; I'll wake you up in a few hours, okay?"

"Sure." He barely smiled before sluggishly wandering to the sofa.

"Paul," Salem said as he came downstairs, "there is a guest bedroom, if you would find that more comfortable. It is the door to the right."

"I've never been in there," I said quietly, suddenly realizing the fact.

"It's nothing compared to ours." He grinned.

Paul somewhat-reluctantly rose from the comfort of the sectional and lumbered up the winding staircase. Once he was out of view, I noticed Salem and I were alone.

"Where is Hannah?" I asked, gazing around the house in case I had somehow missed her.

"She went out ... " he said quietly, uncomfortably.

"She's not out hunting humans, is she?"

"No. She promised she wouldn't ... " He seemed just as doubtful as I had. "She claimed she was saying farewell to Karen."

"What?" I asked in alarm. "Why would she do that?"

"As shocking as it may sound, she said she grew a likeness for her and felt bad at the idea of leaving her without saying goodbye." He almost laughed. "I guess she's never really had a friend before, not even a fake one."

"Saying bye? Is she going somewhere then?" I wondered.

"Hannah isn't leaving, but Claire is ... if that makes sense."

"Yeah, it does."

Salem stared at me for a moment; his eyes clouded with uncertainty, and he briskly pulled me up against him. I found a strange joy in the fact that his skin still felt cold to me, and nestled my head against him. "I truly am worried about you, Alex," he whispered, then parted away slightly to tilt my head up so he could stare into my eyes. "I could never forgive myself if I did anything to harm you, temporarily or otherwise."

"I know," I replied quietly, "but you really shouldn't worry about it ... everything's fine. And besides, even if it wasn't there's no sense in dwelling on it."

With a half-smile, he leaned his head forward and brushed his cool lips against mine—gently at first, then progressively more passionate. I gasped at his touch, the way his hand wove through my hair and tangled it between his fingers. The moment felt infinite and magical—our bodies pressed close together, my heart thumping loudly against his hollow chest, our breath mingling in conjunction with each passing kiss—until the hideous, disgusted shriek broke us apart.

"Yuck! Do you mind?!" Hannah shouted as she came in through the front doors. "I think I'd throw up if I had the ability."

Salem and I rolled our eyes at her. "You are the one who stormed in without knocking," Salem replied, observing his half-sister tearing at the strawberry blonde wig on her head.

Hannah dumped the false hair in the garbage and stared at us. "I told Karen I would see her again sometime. But, don't be surprised if she comes to you in tears in the future, bawling about her distant cousin Claire drowning or dying or something."

"That's horrible," I fumed. "She deserves better than that."

"What's horrible," she interjected, "is whatever I just walked in on." She shuddered.

With a sigh, I plopped myself down on the sectional. I had so much to figure out, and an unspecified amount of time to do it … but I needed Paul to be awake and alert in order for me to even begin.

"I have something for you, Hannah," Salem said, twirling something around in his hand. I glanced at him from the couch and saw the shimmering gold locket.

"Oh!" She gasped with a pleasant smile—it reminded me of when Daniel first presented it to her. "I was certain it was lost forever, until I saw it the day of the picnic—it was really hard not to steal it."

"So I noticed," he replied. "Don't be too surprised if it's not everything you remembered."

"What does that mean?" She shot him a dirty look. "Is it scratched? Did you break it? Is my picture gone?!"

Salem laughed and shook his head, handing the jewelry to her. She examined it closely, turning it around in her hand over and over to check for any damage. When she finally opened the locket her eyes lit up and a joyful expression swept across her face. "Salem … " she whispered, "how?"

"The same way I summon anything else," he said with a satisfied grin. "Do you like it?"

"I love it … "

My curiosity grew stronger with each passing second, and without much thought, I approached them and peeked over Hannah's shoulder. The locket still held the familiar image of the golden-haired child, but the opposite portion of the heart was no longer empty. Instead, it held the image of Daniel—before he became a vampire. I could scarcely stop myself from smiling, despite my hatred for the man. Hannah seemed like a completely different person when she wasn't ravenously hungry, angry, or trying to kill me.

"Have you shown her the pictures upstairs?" I asked.

"No," Salem replied. "Would you like to see them, Hannah?"

The two of them wandered upstairs, leaving me alone in the now quiet living room. I took that opportunity to take advantage of the piano—my piano—once more. How I had not forgotten how to play Nevermore was somewhat of a mystery to me. In fact, I wasn't even quite sure how I came up with it to begin with. But all this time, it was nestled somewhere in the back of my mind just begging to come out, and as soon as my fingers hit those ivory keys it was brought to life again.

My eyes lit up with amazement, and I nearly stopped playing, startled by the alluring, hypnotic sound that I knew must have been coming from the instrument ... however, it sounded different from the tune I remembered so well. I was positive I hit the same exact keys as always, but this song felt and sounded so much stronger, so much more beautiful ...

Was this how it had sounded to Salem when he first heard it? It was no wonder he admired the song so much. This must be how music sounded to a vampire's ears ...

Five hours passed before I saw Paul again. I had grown tired of waiting and went swimming in the lake for about an hour with Salem. I was beyond jealous over the fact that he could remain under water as long as he desired without worrying about coming up for air. I knew it might be possible I could now as well, but there was no way I was going to risk it. Afterward, I took a quick shower and then sat in the nook reading until I watched my father finally appear at the bottom of the stairs.

"Sleep well?" I asked, peeking over the top of the book. He still looked tired.

He shrugged his bulky shoulders. "Could have used more rest, but it'll do for now."

Salem summoned him a bowl of clam chowder by request before departing hastily to feed himself. Hannah was upstairs admiring the photographs again, so I took the time to sit with Paul at the dining room table and discuss meeting my grandfather. I stared at him in silence while he slurped his soup noisily, then as he settled the spoon against the bowl, I opened my mouth to speak.

"I need to call Kate," he said before I had a chance. "Excuse me."

With a groan, I watched him leave the room. Ten minutes more of waiting passed before he returned with a grimace on his face.

"She is having a terrible time over there; I really should get back to work ... but I don't want to leave you."

I nearly laughed. "I'll be fine, dad, really. But, before you go, I have to ask you something."

"Sure, kid," he said and sat back down. "What is it?"

"I want to meet my grandfather," I said after a moment's hesitation.

"He doesn't know you at all, Alex," Paul replied as he slouched in his seat. "He probably doesn't even remember that you exist."

"Well, if he doesn't remember, we can teach him. I need to meet him. He might be my only chance at finding an answer to all this. You said so yourself." My voice was nearly pleading.

"What he tells you might not even be true. He's not all there in the head anymore."

"I thought the same about you and Salem at first when you told me the truth. For all you know, he isn't crazy at all."

Paul sighed. "I just don't want you to get your hopes up for something that may turn up to be nothing but an old crazy man's story. What if he tells you that everything about you is normal, however it turns out to be wrong because he doesn't know for sure, or because he is remembering wrong? Or what if he sends you off on some wild goose chase and gets you hurt, or worse?"

"It's a risk I have to take," I replied stubbornly. "I'd rather have something to go on, even if it turned out to be nothing...rather than just wait around for, whatever, to happen ... "

I could tell he was giving up hope of convincing me otherwise, and I fought the grin that wanted to come out. "His name is Richard Waldron. You can find him at Littlehaven Institute. It's in the next town over, and you will need some sort of proof that you are family. Just ... keep in mind that you can't trust everything he says as the truth, Alex."

"I will," I said, finally letting the grin of success reveal itself. "Thanks, dad."

"You're welcome, I guess." He frowned.

"Go help Kate and then get some more sleep, I'll keep you posted on everything that happens. I promise." We both stood from our seats.

"You had better," he replied, gave me a brief hug and headed toward the door.

Paul nearly bumped into Salem as he was leaving. Neither of them spoke a word to each other as they passed through the doors. Salem greeted me with curious red eyes.. Would I ever grow used to that?

"Where is he off to?" he asked as he embraced me.

"Work," I replied simply. "But before he left I talked him into telling me how to find my grandfather."

Salem let go of me and frowned. "I am not sure it's such a wise decision, Alex ... "

"Oh God, not you, too!" I grumbled. "Whether he is insane or not, I still want to meet him ... even if he doesn't give me the answers at all."

He nodded solemnly. "I understand ... just try not to think too deeply about anything he says to you."

I rolled my eyes at him and set off to check my laptop for more information on Littlehaven. I was relieved to discover there was a web page for the hospital. It was a simple site, with an off-white background and elegant text displaying the institute's name. The front page detailed how pleasant the staff was, how well taken care of the patients were, and all the hospital's amenities. I scrolled through the site until I found what I was looking for. At the very bottom of the page was the word 'Contact Us', which led me to a page with a phone number, fax number, e-mail address, and physical address.

"Salem, paper, please," I said without looking away from the computer screen. Seconds later and there was a piece of paper and a pen on the table beside me. I quickly jotted down the location's address. I was suddenly overwhelmed with excitement and anxiety about the prospect of meeting my grandfather, but I had to hold it back for now.

My next step was to check a map to see just where exactly this hospital was. I found a website that gave directions and input Salem's address and the address to the hospital. "This is going to be a longer trip than I had thought," I said glumly. "Hopefully it's worth it ... "

"We'll be there before you know it, Alex," Salem said comfortingly from behind me. I was glad to know he no longer opposed.

Littlehaven

The following morning, I packed up a few necessities and stuffed them in the Alero before climbing into the driver-side seat. Salem was already waiting for me in the car, scanning the radio for something decent to listen to. I smiled when he stopped at a classical music station. Normally it was always set to that station, but he had let Hannah borrow the vehicle when she went to say goodbye to Karen, and she must have messed around with the radio.

"You think Hannah will behave herself while we are gone?" I asked as I rolled down the windows and pulled out of the garage.

"I trust her enough," Salem replied, a slight edge in his voice, "and I told Paul to keep an eye out ... just in case."

"I am still trying to wrap my mind around the fact that she nearly killed me just a few days ago, and now she is practically living with us." I turned down the winding, long road that led away from the Victorian and directed us toward town. The bumpy roads no longer bothered me; in fact, they were scarcely noticed as we went across.

"You aren't the only one," Salem commented as we drove through the thick forestry, passed the broken down shed and the field of cows.

My eyes veered off of the road temporarily when I noticed something bizarre in the field. I felt sick to my stomach and pulled the car over to the side of the road. Salem didn't seem to quite understand the sudden halt until he glanced at the herd of bovine. They all appeared frightened. "What's wrong with them?" I whispered as I watched a cow topple over into the dry yellow grass. Before I had the opportunity to scream, Salem leaned across the car and put his hand over my mouth. Something—or someone—was crouched down behind the fallen cow.

"This is unexpected … " Salem's expression was blank and unreadable as he scanned the area. "It isn't Hannah," he said quietly, "but they are feeding on animals … "

"A vampire?" I asked as he lowered his hand.

"Yes," he replied, still observing. My eyesight was nothing in comparison to his, even with being part vampire. I could barely make out the shape of a slender woman with long, wavy auburn hair.

"Should I warn Paul?"

He shook his head. "There is no sense in it. She is not hurting anyone—plus, if she does, Paul will know."

"But wouldn't it be better to warn him ahead of time … before someone gets hurt?"

"I don't think she is going to hurt anyone."

"You said the same thing about Mark," I replied harshly.

He looked down and sighed. "You're right."

I called Paul quickly and left him a message about what we had seen, and then drove off toward our destination once more. My mind was wandering as I struggled to keep my eyes on the road. There was another vampire lurking around, and while she may not have been killing humans, that didn't mean she wasn't dangerous. My instincts told me to stay behind and keep watch with Paul, but I didn't know how much time I had. Plus, my dad and aunt could handle the situation ... I hoped.

We drove passed my old high school, where I would have graduated from three weeks prior had I made an effort to stay enrolled. Becoming a vampire hunter had taken away much of my free time, but I wasn't completely displeased with my decision to drop out. There were more important things for me to learn than math, science and English. I had to dedicate my time to learning new fighting techniques and phasing at will. None of the school subjects would have ever prepared me for the life I now had. I spotted Mitchell walking up the sidewalk toward the school doors, but I had no time to stop to say hello.

Next we passed the trailer park my father lived in, an elementary school and a park. I could almost smell the rot of the corpses dwelling beneath the soil as we passed the cemetery. I was relieved to watch it disappear behind us.

Before long, we were in a part of town I wasn't as familiar with. There was a long line of near-identical houses to our right, a gas station to the left, and a school. Noticing at the last moment that the Alero was dangerously low on gas, I veered into the parking lot of the gas station and stopped at a pump. Salem looked shocked at first but then the reason for our stop dawned on him. How he had lived all these years and still shunned most technology I will never know. I popped open the console and took out some of the remains of what used to be a completely full envelope. As I did a pain shot through my body, deep into my heart. I hadn't thought much about Janet...about my mom...in quite some time. I felt a pang of guilt as I pulled what little money was left from what she had left me, and exited the car.

The cashier seemed friendly enough, maybe too friendly. He was perhaps sixteen, with light, curly red hair and a face covered in freckles. Ralph, as his nametag told me, must have been pretty lonely out here in this little gas station. After much effort, I drug myself away from whatever conversation he was attempting to make and headed out. After filling the tank with gas, I hopped back into the car.

Salem immediately gave me a strange look. "What took you so long?"

"What? Oh. Nothing, the cashier was just a little lonely was all."

"I see."

"You're not seriously jealous are you?" I rolled my eyes. I knew Salem had been a little skeptical about my relationship with Jason at first, but this was a stranger.

"No. Let's just go."

I didn't even bother replying as I shifted into drive and pulled out of the parking lot back onto the road. Within ten minutes, we met the highway and began our journey out of town toward Littlehaven Institute.

What was I even going to say to my grandfather when I met him? I turned my attention briefly to Salem, who was staring out the window and watching the world go by. "Salem?" I said quietly, my eyes set upon the road ahead once more.

"Yes?"

"I thought of something that's kind of been bothering me a little."

"What is it?" he asked. I could see him staring at me from the corner of my eye.

"What if my grandfather is dead or not living at the institute anymore?" I said, trying to hold back the panic.

"If he were dead, Paul would have been informed," he insisted. "And if he isn't at the hospital for some reason, I am sure someone there can direct us to where he has relocated to."

"You're right," I said, attempting a smile.

Roughly thirty miles into our trip, we pulled into a rest stop so that I could use the bathroom. Salem summoned me a sandwich, which I ate despite my lack of appetite, and its lack of taste. Then back on the road we went, following the crude directions I had written down from the Internet. After twenty miles more, we still had not reached Littlehaven. According to the directions I had gotten, we should have been there almost ten miles ago. After continuing on for a couple of miles Salem suggested we stop somewhere and ask if we were still headed the right way. I pulled over at the first available place, a tiny inn.

As I entered I was greeted with little more than a nod from a middle-aged Asian man. "Hi, would you be able to help us? We're trying to get to Littlehaven. The directions I wrote down said it should be around here close by, are we almost there?"

The man pushed his thick horn-rimmed glasses up his nose and stared at me for a minute. At first I thought he may not speak English, but then he opened his mouth. "Littlehaven, you say? You are a long way off. It's southwest of here. Exit is maybe, forty miles south still."

"Forty miles south?!" I exclaimed. We had passed the exit almost forty miles ago? "Are you sure that is where it is? You see I'm trying to get to-"

"Yes, yes I am sure. Do you need a room or no?"

"What? No. Thank you." I left the inn irritated, more so with the knowledge of how far we had gone off track than with the rude innkeeper.

"So, how far do we need to go still?" Salem asked with a genuine curious look on his face.

I let out a small frustrated scream. "He says we passed the exit like two hours ago."

"What?"

"Yeah. I don't know how. I guess I wrote down the directions wrong in my excitement, I don't know." I slammed my fist into the steering wheel and grunted again.

"Alex, it will be okay. It is barely passed one o'clock. We still have plenty of time to get there today."

As he spoke I suddenly became overcome by exhaustion. How could this even be possible? I had slept a full day, then the night after had gotten a complete normal night's sleep. I had only been up maybe five hours. Salem must have noticed my sudden weakness.

"Alex, are you okay? You look...pale."

"Yeah, I'm fine. Just a little tired all of a sudden." My head nodded over and for a moment I thought I was going to fall asleep where I sat. How could I be so tired?

"Nonsense. We are at an inn, let's just go inside and stay a while."

"No, I'm fine. We need to go. I have to find my grandfather."

"Littlehaven will still be there tomorrow. I'm worried about you Alex, and if you are tired, you should rest. Now, let's get inside."

I looked up as we entered the little office of the inn, seeing the Asian man with a look of pure annoyance.

"Look. I told you, Littlehaven is south on highway. Exit on right side."

"We need a room," Salem said simply.

"Oh, a room, okay. Yes. We have eight rooms. Six open right now. Two have nice view of-"

"Any room is fine. It doesn't matter. We just need some rest from our travel."

"Okay, very well, here is key. Room number seven, around back and near end. Okay?"

After paying for a single night of use, we walked off to find our room.

It was small and cramped, but I didn't care at the moment. I groggily lay across the full-sized bed without bothering to change into something more comfortable. I felt Salem slip my shoes off and drape a blanket across me that hadn't previously existed moments earlier. Sleep came over me quicker than I had anticipated, but I welcomed it happily.

I woke to find that it was surprisingly the following morning. How I had slept so long again was a mystery, but I soon forgot about my thoughts as I was presented with a bowl of cereal. It was the simplest meal Salem had ever prepared for me, but I wasn't complaining. I spooned every last piece of cereal into my mouth and set the bowl aside. I was fortunate that my body was still capable of digesting human food, despite its near tastelessness. Blood simply was not something I had any interest in ever consuming again. After I had eaten I took a quick shower. I was surprised that Salem was nowhere to be seen.

I headed towards the office to go ahead and check out, making sure to grab a little travel map from a shelf inside before I headed for the car. When I got there, Salem was sitting on the hood.

"I guess that means you are ready to go now, then?" I laughed.

"Are you? I have been worried about how tired you have been getting lately, Alex, but I think I may know why."

"Oh, really?"

"Yes. I know you are not a complete vampire, but you are also not fully human. I think the reason you have been so tired is your lack of sustenance."

"What? You mean food? But I've been eating plenty. That doesn't make any sense really. Yesterday I had just eaten that sandwich before-"

"No," he cut me off, "I mean sustenance for the vampiric part of you."

"What are you talking...wait...you mean blood, don't you?! No way! I am not doing that again unless I have to."

"Exactly my point, I think you *have to*."

"But you don't know for sure. Look, I feel fine right now, let's just go."

"Very well, but next time you are randomly exhausted for no reason, we need to try it."

"Whatever."

We pulled out and headed south towards the exit we had somehow missed before. Salem appeared deep in thought, barely making even small talk during the car ride.

"Is something on your mind?" I asked as we passed a long pasture spotted with the occasional horse.

"I am just wondering what Richard will say about your ... condition," he replied distantly.

"Oh," I said quietly, thinking now on the same subject. For all I knew, this would be a complete waste of time, and my grandfather wouldn't know any more about it than Paul,

Salem, or myself. Of course, when I factored in that I would be meeting my grandfather for the first time, and that made it slightly less pointless if nothing else came of the visit. As I thought this over, we drove ever-nearer to our destination.

We got to the exit before I knew it. The trip hadn't felt nearly as long this time. I turned right and shook my head as I realized how we had missed the turn before. The street sign lay on the ground, knocked over by who knows what. I was just glad we were finally on track. We had barely twenty more miles before we would arrive at Littlehaven.

Without taking any stops, we arrived at the town before long, if that is what you would call it. I thought Willowshire had been small, but this was Everything looked old, and everything was spread out. No one seemed to have an actual neighbor here; the houses were, for the most part, separated by several acres of land.

Luckily, my directions to the location of the mental hospital had been accurate, and after a few turns here and there I could see the large brick building up ahead, surrounded by a thick wrought-iron fence. I drove slowly into the parking lot, checking to make sure I didn't park someplace reserved, then finally chose a spot. I felt like hours had passed while I sat there staring at the building. It was four stories, with barred windows on the upper levels. There was a field of green grass surrounding the front, and potted plants with various colorful flowers aligning a thin walkway that led to the entrance. About ten feet in front of the building was a stone fountain with a waterfall, and atop it was a cement sign with the name 'Littlehaven Institute' across it in big, bold letters. Why they had chosen this little speck of a town for this large hospital, I wasn't sure.

I could faintly hear Salem saying my name, and I turned to look at him. "Are you okay?"

"Yeah, I'm fine," I muttered. "Just a little nervous. That's all."

"Don't be," he said reassuringly. "There's nothing to be anxious about, and I will be with you the whole time."

I attempted to smile as I left the car and met him on the opposite side. He took my hand and gripped it tightly, reassuringly, and we approached the wrought-iron gate. Salem pushed it open, and it creaked noisily on its hinges. I felt more like I was headed toward a prison than a mental hospital, which only increased my anxiety.

The rippling water in the fountain was clear and beautiful, trickling down slowly into a pool filled with shimmering coins. Soon our feet met the thin pathway, and I could smell the floral aroma coming off of the plants as we passed them. The smell was so strong it was nearly sickening. I took a deep breath when we approached the two doors, and before I had the chance to turn back, Salem had his hands around the handle and was opening it.

Grandpa Waldron

    We were met immediately by a welcoming breeze that tickled my skin, and I noticed a cooling vent blowing air down from the ceiling. The floor was covered in light green marble tile, aside from the thick black mats we stood on. To the left was a receptionist's desk, and to the right was a row of roughly thirty chairs, a vending machine and a small television perched up on the wall. Behind the desk was a slender, pleasant-looking woman with slightly graying copper hair that she wore up in a neat bun. I cautiously walked up to the desk, and she stared at me expectantly through thin-rimmed spectacles. She reminded me all too much of a librarian.

    It took me a moment to find my voice, and when I finally did it came out hoarse and mumbled, "I'm here to see a patient."

    "Excuse me?" she said, her voice was somewhat impatient.

    "I'm sorry," I said as I cleared my throat. "I am here to see a patient."

    "Who might you be seeing?"

"Richard Waldron," I said with more confidence.

She eyed me awkwardly, and then arched a brow. "Are you sure you have the right name?"

My heart sunk. My assumptions must have been right—he wasn't here anymore; this was a complete waste of time, and I was never going to get any answers.

"Yes, she is," Salem answered for me.

"No one has ever come to visit Mr. Waldron before," she said in awe.

So, maybe I was wrong.

"Are you a relative?"

"Yes, I'm his granddaughter," I replied.

"Name, please?"

"Alexis Waldron. Or, it might be listed as Hobbs."

She nodded and glanced at the computer monitor in front of her. I heard her fingers typing on the keyboard as she looked up the information. "You are indeed listed as his granddaughter," she said. "Looks like someone called in to add you just yesterday. I will have a nurse sent down to take you to his room."

"Thanks ... " I said quietly as Salem and I retreated to the opposite side of the room and sat in the waiting area. The TV was so tiny that I could barely make out the pictures on the screen, and it was muted. There was a stack of magazines on a small table in the corner of the room, but I was never too fond of reading those. I was just glad Paul had apparently remembered to call and add me to the family listing.

"Relax, Alex," Salem whispered, holding both of my hands now. I hadn't noticed how much I was fidgeting until then. "You have nothing to be worried about."

"I have a lot to be worried about."

"No, you don't," he insisted. "Trust me."

Just as I was about to reply again, a short, rotund man with thick, curly ginger hair came through two doors I had previously not noticed. They were to the left of the receptionist desk, leading down a long hallway. He was wearing dark-blue scrubs with pictures of fish on the shirt. He said my name as he came through the swinging doors, and I hesitantly got up.

"You are here to see Mr. Waldron?" he asked in a quiet, boyish voice.

"I am," I replied. Salem and I followed him through the white doors. We walked down the hallway, passing a restroom and two doors, one of which read "Employees Only", then came upon an elevator and a staircase.

The nurse—whose name tag read "John"—clicked the up arrow beside the elevator doors, and we stood in silence, waiting. The doors slid open, and the three of us entered. I felt increasingly more nervous the closer we got to the top floor, and was positive I was going to throw up when the doors flew open. Salem gripped my hand tightly again as we walked onto the white, glossy linoleum floor of the upper level. I swallowed back the oncoming bile and examined my new surroundings.

We were in the center of a long, wide room. I could see some of the barred windows overlooking the backside of the building. All that I could see through them was a set of patio furniture and even more grass. At the very end of the room, to our left, were another small television and a wooden table. On the table lay a pile of three or four board game boxes; two patients sat playing cards in the little uncovered space. To the right was a wall of closed doors on each side, another restroom, and at the very end there appeared to be a turn that undoubtedly led to even more rooms.

"Mr. Waldron is one of our more eccentric patients," John said as he led us down the hall of doors and around the bend. "He has been with us for several years without a visitor, which is a shame. He seems like a nice enough man, even if the things he says are a little off the wall sometimes. I am his usual nurse, and even though he talks about supernatural things all the time, he never seems to be quite as ... loopy ... as the rest of the folks here."

"I don't believe he is crazy at all," I replied. "If you ask me, it was all a misunderstanding."

"You might change your mind after you meet him. Like I said, he is nice and seems stable, but he does talk about some strange stuff," the man said, stopping abruptly at a door with the number "33 D" etched into the wood. There was a small peep hole below the digits. John knocked lightly and waited for a response.

Now was the time to really panic. My grandfather was behind this door. What was he going to be like? Would he like me, would he approve of Salem? "Oh, no ... " I gasped in realization.

"What's the matter?" John asked, eying me curiously.

"It's nothing," I said, although both the nurse and Salem were aware that I was lying. I could feel sweat trickling down my forehead. There was no doubt in my mind that my grandfather would recognize Salem for what he was. I was a fool to have brought him here! "S-Salem ... do you think you could wait out here, until I've talked to him a little?"

"Of course," he replied. "I understand."

He smiled and despite his eagerness to please me, it almost made me feel worse. Salem stepped aside and leaned against the wall near the door. I heard the door creak open and unintentionally stared at the man before me—he returned the gaze.

"Afternoon, Richard," John said calmly, smiling warmly at the old man. "You have a visitor!"

The old man standing in the doorway looked surprisingly familiar. His eyes were so much like Kim's; it was uncanny. It was hard to believe he was Paul's father, considering how tall and bulky Paul was, whereas this man was short, maybe my height, and gauntly thin. He wore gray sweat pants and a plain white T-shirt that hung loosely around his brittle frame. There was receding gray and bronze hair atop his scalp, and I would have guessed he was in his mid-sixties or late seventies. He looked stern, cautious and also curious.

"Who is she?" he asked in a suspicious voice, directed toward John.

"You may have trouble believing this, but she is listed as your granddaughter," the nurse replied. "Your son's kid."

My grandfather's eyes sunk and he shook his head in disbelief. "Paul told me he couldn't handle taking care of a kid after that wife of his died, and put her up for adoption."

"Well, she's found you somehow; she's on the list," John replied with somewhat of a pleased smile.

"Paul's actually the one who sent me here," I finally spoke, and our eyes met again.

"Hm," the old man said and suddenly smiled. "You do look a lot like Destiny."

"Paul...dad...told me the same," I replied awkwardly. I wish I had gotten the opportunity to know the woman that gave birth to me. "I was hoping we could have some time to chat."

"Of course. That would be great," he said, then looked at John. "Could I have my hour of outdoor time now instead of the usual?"

"Of course," the nurse said and smiled. "I'll come get you when time is up."

I watched John walk down the linoleum toward the elevator and disappear. "Where did you have in mind?" I asked.

"I usually spend it out on the lawn," Richard replied. "But first, if you don't mind ... " He reached his frail arms out and hugged me. "You cannot imagine how long I have waited for this day."

I laughed gingerly and hugged him back. "I didn't even know you existed until a few days ago ... but I'm happy to know you do."

He smiled a big, toothy grin and took my hand. I no longer felt quite as nervous, until we turned to walk away from the door, and I knew Salem would be standing there. But, as I turned around I was shocked to find the area vacant. Where could he have gone? I hoped quietly that my grandfather didn't notice the look of displeasure.

We walked slowly across the room, and I was once again enveloped in the tiny elevator box. I hit the button for the first floor and waited as we went down. The doors opened, and we were in the lobby. Another set of doors that I had not noticed the first time were revealed at the back of the waiting room area.

"This leads out back," the old man said and pushed them open.

We walked to the patio furniture and sat down. I noticed this was not the only set of furniture; there were at least four others along the field. There were other patients outside, all of them supervised by a nurse. I noticed with excitement and understanding that Salem was out here—not only could I smell him, but I could see his distinct shape among a row of rose bushes up against the fence that enclosed the place. He must have heard Richard's request and rushed out here ahead of us.

"So tell me about you," the old man said eagerly, leaning across the table and perching his head on his hands.

"There isn't much to tell really." I shrugged. "I'm just Alex...your average teenager ... with a twist." I grimaced.

"Paul talked you into being a hunter," he stated, no hint of questioning in his voice. "It's a shame. He lost his wife and mother to it, and now he's risking his daughter, too."

"It was my choice," I said in Paul's defense. "I sort of didn't have much other option."

"What do you mean?" He stared inquisitively at me.

"I'm sure you have heard rumor of some of our ancestors being able to become ravens ... " I spoke quietly, with my head down.

To my surprise, he slammed a fist against the table. "Nonsense!"

"No, it's true ... "

He shook his head. "No, I believe that, what I don't believe is that he could get you into this mess ... willingly!"

"I had my reasons, trust me."

"There are no good enough reasons to do this by choice." He frowned at me, making his wrinkles more evident. "Why'd you come here anyway? Just letting me know I had another relative who's bound to get themselves killed?"

"No...I wanted to come and tell you that I don't think you're crazy, and I don't believe that you deserve to be here," I said, avoiding his question.

He smiled. "I want to be here, regardless if I truly need to be or not. It protects me from them, and from my urge to go hunting still."

"You ... you want people to think you are insane?"

"I don't so much like that part of it, but it is so freeing!" He laughed giddily. "That is why I had Veronica Dillard convince everyone I had attacked her."

I stared at him in disbelief. "Veronica Dillard? Who is that?"

"She was an old friend of your grandmother's. She thinks the reason I wanted admitted here was because I was grieving over Samantha's death and wanted to be taken care of, and that I had some underlying issues with depression ... which isn't entirely a lie."

Samantha—I wondered what my grandmother had been like, it was almost as troubling as never knowing my real mother.

"Paul thinks you are crazy, and fears you aren't the person he used to know ... that is why he never visits."

He shrugged. "I'm not surprised. It might be better that way. The less involvement I have with vampires and hunting, the better."

I sighed, and he noticed the dissatisfied look on my face. "I guess I might have come out here for nothing, then."

"What did you come all this way for, Alex? I don't believe for a second it was just to meet me." His voice had grown serious.

"I'm not entirely who you think I am...or what you think I am."

He eyed me with a curious arch of his shaggy graying eyebrows. "Well, you're not a vampire; that's for sure. So what are you talking about? Spit it out."

"No. I'm not a vampire, but I'm not ... " I exhaled slowly. "I'm not completely human, either, and you may be the only one that can help me ... "

Old Friends

    Richard leapt up from his seat at a speed faster than I thought humanly possible for someone his age. He looked bewildered, an expression of horror plastered across his paling face. One of the nurses looked in our direction, and I prayed they wouldn't react to his behavior and come inspect the situation.

    "You've been bitten," he said flatly, his limbs shaking.

    I slowly nodded in response. "Yes."

    "This can't be. You should be either dead, or one of those beasts." He began pacing nervously around the table. "When did it happen?"

    "Almost a week ago."

    "And you still aren't one of those monsters?" I hated the way he spoke the last word; it sickened me. "This is very interesting ... very interesting."

    "What is?" I asked, and the anxiety returned.

    "I don't know how much time we have to discuss this, and not only because I am on the clock." He stopped pacing and stared at me with a grim expression. "If I had the equipment, I think it would be wisest that I killed you here and now."

Through the corner of my eye, I could see Salem turn in our direction. He must have heard Richard. "That's nonsense ... I'm not a vampire, as you can plainly see ... "

"*Yet*," he replied through gritted teeth. "You probably don't have much longer; it usually doesn't take this long."

"Well that's sort of why I'm here, I-"

Before I could get any more out, he had interrupted me. "There's a lot I need to tell you, child." Richard fumbled around in his pants pocket. He offered a small, crumpled up piece of paper to me. "Call this number, and maybe we can meet again soon—very soon. Mention how urgent it is."

I had no opportunity to question my grandfather, as John approached us unexpectedly from behind. "It's time to return indoors, Richard," he said casually. "I'm sorry to take you from your first visitor, but you know the rules. I'm sure she can come back again soon."

"Hopefully so," my grandfather replied, gave me a sorrowful look and turned away with the nurse.

Salem was beside me in mere seconds, glancing at the piece of paper the old man had given to me. I wondered how long it had been in his pocket. The letters and digits were barely legible, but I could make out the name. That might be enough; I could look the number up online if need be. "Is this the woman who accused him of attacking her?" Salem asked.

"Veronica ... I wonder what part she plays in all this. Do you think she has more to do with it than just the story about him being put in here?" I let out a long sigh. "This hasn't been very helpful at all."

"You don't know that yet, Alex. Maybe this woman will be of some benefit to us."

"Maybe ... " I replied doubtfully and stuffed the note into my hoodie pocket.

My grandfather had acted so strange after finding out I was bitten. Part of me wondered if he was a little crazy after all these years here with the other patients, or at least a little senile. The first second he wanted to kill me outright, the next he seemed to want to see me again and tell me something important. I wondered if he had really told me the whole story of Veronica and his fake attack.

The ride home was a little more tolerable this time, mostly due to the fact I knew I wouldn't get lost going home. As night fell we were back in our familiar surroundings. I was relieved to see the cemetery, the high school, the trailer park. I decided to stop to see if Paul was home, but no one answered the door, so we rode over to the auto shop.

Kate was as friendly as ever, greeting me with much enthusiasm, although she looked very bored and exhausted behind the counter. She let me know she was on her way home, and jabbered off some more small talk before she headed out the door. Salem had come in with me, following behind as if he were my shadow. I found Paul in his usual place, the back room behind his desk.

"Alexis!" He beamed, setting down his pen and yellow pad. "So, how was the trip?"

"It was ... interesting. I didn't really get what I was looking for, but I still have a few ideas."

"Has there been any word on that unfamiliar vampire?" Salem piped in.

"There haven't been any sightings that I've heard of yet. Kim and I scouted around the pasture, as well as around the Victorian—just in case. We could definitely tell something had been there though, and there have been a few reports on some livestock mutilations. Hell, someone in the shop earlier was talking about one of his cows and said it must have been aliens; it took all I had not to laugh."

"Interesting," Salem said. "It must be the vampire we saw and told you about. There haven't been any mysterious death reports or such? Either in town or nearby towns?"

"Just one, but Kim isn't entirely convinced it was a vampire attack. It was way too brutal."

"Do I even want to know?" I asked with a grimace.

"Probably not."

"I didn't think so. Sorry to cut this short, I just wanted to stop by on the way back home and let you know we saw grandpa. I have some things I need to do ... "

"Such as?" He stared at me curiously, and I gave him the full report on what Richard had told me, but he was still skeptical about whether or not his father was sane.

Salem and I immediately went home after leaving the auto shop. It was a huge relief to be surrounded by the familiar gray walls, the sectional sofa, and the window overlooking the lake. I smiled to myself as I walked into the living room and draped myself across the couch. There was little time to relax as Salem offered me one of the cell phones we possessed and told me I should call Veronica; I was honestly dreading it. What would I even say to her? My grandfather hadn't given me any clues.

Luckily, I thought of a legitimate excuse to delay the call, and give me some more time to think of what exactly I would say. It had gotten pretty late during the hours of driving home from Littlehaven, and I was sleepy. Besides, Veronica must have been old as well; she was probably in bed herself.

When I told Salem about being tired, he gave me an alarmed look. "Alex, do you need to eat? Are you exhausted again?"

"No, relax. I'm fine, just sleepy. Let's get some rest; I'll call first thing in the morning, promise."

Salem took me up on my word quite literally. As soon as I opened my eyes he handed me my cell phone. Reluctantly, I rose from the bed and took it from his cold hand. I pulled out the wrinkled paper from my pocket and attempted to input it in the phone, praying the numbers were right. The phone rang three times.

"No one's answering," I said, letting it continue ringing.

"Give it a while longer," he suggested, now sitting beside me.

I nodded my head and waited. Five rings. Six. I nearly jumped when I heard the scratchy voice from the other end.

"Hello?" she repeated.

"Hi ... " My voice came out quieter than I intended. "Is this Veronica Dillard?"

"Yes, who's this?"

"This is Alexis Waldron, Richard's granddaughter ... he told me I should call you, that you might be able to help me."

There was a pause before she spoke again. "He told me I might expect a call from a relative someday," she replied with a gentle wisp of laughter.

Although she could not see it, my eyes furrowed in confusion. "Why'd he tell you that?"

"Richard believed that someday he might need me to set the truth straight on the attack, in hopes that the hospital might let him out," the old lady replied. "I must say, I was not expecting it to ever happen. After Sam's passing, I thought he might decide to stay in there for good."

"It's kind of desperate that he gets out as soon as possible," I said hastily. "If you are able, we would both really appreciate it if there was any way you could convince the Institute that you were wrong, and he's not crazy."

"You must really want him out of there."

"Yes. I only just recently figured out he even exists, and I don't want him to spend the rest of his life stuck in that hospital," I explained. "It's a nice place and all, and he does enjoy it, but now that he knows he has more family out here, he wants out. I think he is finally over Sam...my grandmother's...death."

"I understand. I'll see what I can do, but I can't make any promises."

"Thank you so much, Veronica. You don't know how much this means to us!" I replied joyously. "Please call me as soon as you figure anything out, it's really important to me that he gets out of there."

I waited patiently for the elder woman to find a pen and paper, and then passed along my number to her. My doubts were high that she would be able to do anything; after all, my grandpa had been pretending to be crazy for several years while being in the institute. For all I knew they could think he had somehow contacted Veronica to get out before he was really ready. I tried to shake the thoughts from my head and stay positive, but wondered how long it would be before I heard back from Veronica...or if I would at all.

Changes

    Two nights had passed before I was woken up at six in the morning by the sound of my phone ringing. It took a lot of effort to get myself to pick it up, and I scarcely noticed Salem's absence as I answered the phone. The familiar scratchy voice was on the other end, followed by some muffled voices in the background. "Alexis?"

    "Yeah?" I replied groggily, wiping at my tired eyes.

    "I'm sorry if I woke you, but I wanted to deliver the news as soon as possible," Veronica said cheerfully. "There's someone here that would like to talk to you."

    I waited as she passed the phone to someone else, and my heart rate quickened at the sound of Richard's voice. "It worked, Alex! It worked!" he exclaimed into the receiver. "I'm free!"

    "What? That's awesome! Where are you now?" I asked, the excitement overlapping the exhaustion temporarily.

    "Paul is driving Veronica and me into town. He's going to drop her off at her house, then we're coming to see you."

HYBRID

My voice failed me at the mentioning of my father. How had he become involved? "Paul's with you?" I asked in a dumbstruck voice.

"Veronica convinced him to come along. She used to babysit him when he was a kid. She can't drive, as she's partially blind and asked him to be her ride," Richard stated. "We should be there in a few short hours."

"How long have you been out?"

"Just now. It was a shorter process than I'd have thought. The day after you left they took me into a room and asked me if what Veronica said was true, and I agreed. Then they did some tests, and evaluations, and with a good boost from my nurse, John, telling them I have seemed fine for many months now…they agreed to let me go."

"Well, I can say for sure that I'm surprised too,." I laughed tiredly.

"I just have to see the doc up there again once a month for a while, and bi-monthly they will do a home visit to make sure everything seems right. Standard procedure of course, I've never had anything wrong with me."

"Well, it's worth it to be out I think, even with that."

"Well dear, I'll see you soon; I'm going to get off here and catch up a little with Paul if he'll let me." I heard Paul laugh a little in the background; I was glad he seemed okay with all this.

"Okay, see you soon, bye." We both hung up, and I curled back up under the covers. It still hadn't completely dawned on me that Salem wasn't beside me. Sleep came over me quickly, and I slept for the next two hours, until finally he came into the room.

"Alex?" I heard his accented voice whispering right beside my ear. "Are you awake?"

• • •

"I am now," I replied playfully and turned over to look at him. The crimson rings around his pupils didn't bother me for a change. "You've been out hunting I see?"

"Hannah asked for my help. She wanted me to show her how to properly hunt an animal," he explained. "She still isn't very satisfied with the change in her diet, but promises to continue trying."

"Well, that's good … " The fact that Hannah was adapting to her new lifestyle was comforting, but I still couldn't trust her completely. If it hadn't been for Salem, either she or I would be dead by now, possibly both.

"Did you sleep well?" He caressed my face delicately with his cold palm, admiring me affectionately.

"Yes. Wait!" I gasped and sat up, ruining the near-perfect moment. Turning over and reaching for my phone from on top of the nightstand, I glanced at the recent call list. The memories from earlier this morning came rushing through my mind. It hadn't been a dream. "We're having guests any minute!"

"We are?" He arched a brow and eyed the electronic device I held. "Why? Who?"

"My dad and grandpa are on their way here!" I shook my head in disbelief and frustration, realizing how unprepared we were. "Hannah needs to leave the house while they're here. I know you trust her, and she may be getting better, but I'm not sure she can handle the smell of three humans in the house yet."

Salem frowned. "If it makes you more comfortable, then I will ask her to leave."

"And you … you have to make yourself scarce at least to begin with. Richard might go ballistic if he discovers I'm living with a vampire. At least let Paul and I try to explain it to him first. You know, ease him into it if we can."

"Of course." His frown ceased to fade. "How long have we got?"

"Not long, they had just left there two hours ago. They had to stop at Veronica's, but that's probably it."

He nodded and left the room. I placed my phone back on the nightstand and climbed out of bed. The walk-in closet at the end of the massive bedroom was filled with clothing that Salem had materialized for me, and I was eager to try on something different. Most days I would stick with the typical jeans and a blouse, but today I opted for a black silk shirt and a matching knee-high skirt that perfectly framed my body. If my days were indeed limited, I might as well enjoy them, right? The outfit definitely reflected the raven in me, which no longer made me uncomfortable.

I admired my reflection briefly in the bathroom mirror, flattering myself with what I saw. As I was turning away, something caught my attention. The fact that my complexion had grown slightly paler than before was not startling, but the apparent change in color of my hair nearly made me scream. Where had the mundane locks of brunette disappeared to? A flowing mess of ebony fell across my shoulders, tinted with streaks of radiant purples. How had Salem not noticed this?

"Salem!" I called in horror, tugging at the unfamiliar strands of hair. This had to have been a trick he was playing on me, or maybe Hannah was the culprit. Whatever it was, it needed to be fixed before my relatives got here!

There was scarcely any noise as Salem rushed up the stairs and into the bathroom. He gawked at me from outside the doorway, apparently oblivious to the cause. "Alex … what happened to your hair?"

"I was hoping you could tell me!"

He stepped into the room, standing directly beside me and admired the difference. "Your hair almost perfectly mirrors the colors of the raven's feather," he whispered in awe, fingering through the unnatural strands. "Maybe Richard will have an answer for you."

I shook my head, watching the black hair twirl magnificently with the movement. It was hard to stop myself, but I had to admit that I liked the change. "This doesn't even make sense. Why would my hair just change? It wasn't like this just a minute ago when you were up here?"

"No, it wasn't. I wish I knew what it meant, Alex." He frowned, then eyed me up and down and smiled. "You look lovely, by the way."

"Thanks." I returned the smile. Before I had the opportunity to say anymore, I heard the melodic doorbell. "Is Hannah gone?!" I asked in a worried voice.

"She is," he confirmed, "and I will stay up here until you need me."

"I always need you." I smiled and kissed him gently before heading down the stairs.

Needless to say, Paul and Richard were both startled by the sudden change in my hair. While I had been hopeful to meet Veronica, it was probably wisest that she wasn't present. My grandfather was amazed by the Victorian—as everyone was that ever came to visit—and found it hard to believe my foster mother had been capable of affording such a massive, beautiful piece of architecture. I wondered how he was going to react to the truth behind how I came to live here.

"So...how are you two...you know?" I asked quietly to Paul as Richard examined the house.

He nodded. "I already apologized for how I acted, and not visiting and all, and he said he understood completely.

He is really interested in you, Alex...scared, but very curious nonetheless."

"What is he scared of?" I asked with a frown, although I was pretty positive I knew the reason.

"You are so unusual, in so many ways. You should be dead right now or at least undead ... but you're not. We had a little bit of time to talk between Veronica's house and here, and he does have some ideas though."

"Like what?"

"Like that I'm starving! Your dad there wouldn't stop for nothing!" Richard said and eyed the kitchen eagerly. I stared at him awkwardly, then realized he was about to be greatly disappointed by the lack of food in the fridge. But as he pulled the door open, we were both stunned. The shelves were neatly organized with various food items. The wrinkled hand of my grandfather reached into the fridge and gathered all the ingredients necessary to make a ham sandwich. "Your daughter is awfully tidy," he commented toward Paul as he made his lunch. "Sure didn't get it from you. If you'd have cleaned something when you were a teenager I'd have had a heart attack."

My father laughed and glanced at me nervously.

"It's a surprise you haven't moved in here with her. It's a much nicer place than that old dump you live in," he paused and spread some mustard across a slice of bread, "you do still live in that little old trailer, don't you?"

Paul grumbled under his breath and shook his head. "My home is everything I need."

"You just don't want to leave it cause that's where you and *she* lived," Richard said, looking up and frowning at my father. "Destiny is gone, and you need to let that go son."

"Just like you have let mom go ... "

The old man pursed his lips and quietly went back to his sandwich preparation. He gathered a plate from one of the many mahogany cabinets—after looking through each of them until he finally came across the right one—then sat at the dining table. Paul and I followed suit and sat in uncomfortable silence as Richard delved into his meal.

"So, where are you planning to go now that you are out of Littlehaven?" I asked suddenly.

"My old house," he replied. "Your grandmother and I lived together in a little cottage on the other side of town, in another part of the woods. It was really peaceful out there, aside from the occasional vampire or two, you know."

"The vampire population must be awfully enormous. I can't believe how many are around here … "

"You would be amazed at how many vampires are out in our world, kid," Paul grumbled. "There are some who live in groups—families, as they like to call themselves—and then there are the solo kinds. Either way I think there is something that draws them around these parts. Maybe it's all the nature and places to hide...who knows."

"Families? Well, I'm glad I haven't run into any families," I replied in shock. "Two of them at once were bad enough."

"You two sure are ruining my appetite," Richard said as he bit into his sandwich.

"This is what we brought you here for … to talk about vampires, or at least half-vampires."

I shuddered involuntarily at Paul's words as I awaited a response from my grandfather. All I could do now was hope that he had an answer for me, even if it was as simple as "there is nothing anyone can do for you now".

History

Richard finished his sandwich and pushed aside the crumb-covered saucer before staring across the table at me. He crossed his hands, resting them gently on the table and studying me from afar. I felt awkward as we sat in silence, wondering just what he was going to say.

"I am about to tell you the history of the Waldron bloodline," he finally said, his gaze never faltering. "Are you ready for it?"

"I think so," I replied with a hint of interest, still not entirely sure how this would help solve my problem.

"Your father has never heard it either," he commented, finally looking away from me to glance at his son. "Are you ready to hear it too, Paul?"

"I don't see why not," he said, bitterness from the last conversation still evident in his voice.

Richard cleared his throat and flexed his thin, bony fingers. "The Waldron line has existed since the late-17th century, although vampires existed long before then, of course. The very first hunter was a man named Walter Ravensly—whom eventually was given the nickname of

'Waldron', meaning 'strong raven'," he explained, then requested a glass of water. I hesitantly left my seat and poured him a beverage and returned to my spot. "Thank you, Alexis." He took a long gulp of water before resuming his story. "Vampires and hunters alike weren't as secretive or unheard of back then. It was common to discuss the undead among friends, family, and even strangers. They were vile, untamed creatures that killed with no concern for their victims—not too different from the vampires of today. Back then, you could go to just about any local store and find at least a crude vampire slaying kit.

"Walter Ravensly married and his wife gave birth to their only child. He passed on his nickname of Waldron to his newborn son Thomas, rather than Ravensly. Thomas Waldron was one of the first and few hunters capable of transforming into a raven, or so they say. He was unfortunately accused of witchery and burned at the stake. Even his father was convinced that this was evidence of black magic, and he felt little remorse over the loss of his son. Before his death, however, Thomas had wed and sired two children—Agatha and William Waldron, neither of which possessed any kind of ability to speak of.

"Nearly a century passed before another Waldron discovered his ability to transform. Clarence, however, was wise enough to keep the secret between himself and his closest friends. Three generations after Clarence and the third Waldron with the ability was born—Joseph. He, too, married and had two children—Richard and Carolyn. Joseph was discovered murdered a few years after his children were born—no doubt to the work of a vampire." He scowled and looked down at the tabletop for a moment.

"Female hunters were unheard of until the 20th century, and as far as anyone has ever known ... no Waldron girl had been born with the gift. Vampires became less and less seen and spoken of as the years went on. They learned to adapt with the times and became stealthy hunters. Ordinary folk speak of them like they're myths nowadays, and criminals are blamed for most of their attacks."

"Joseph," I whispered. "He was your father?"

Richard smiled, "You're pretty quick with your math there, kid. Yes, Joseph was your great grandfather. Carolyn didn't live more than a few months from birth, sadly; otherwise, I believe she might still be here today." His smile faded to a frown once more. "But anyway, there are two reasons I told you two this history. The first is that it seems every third third-generation is born with the gift. My dad had the gift, your dad and I don't. Which means you might have the gift, Alex. I know I said no women have had it before, that we know of anyway, but you might."

"Grandpa ... "

"Just hear me out, Alex. I think it might be possible, with the right mindset and some training, for you to become a raven."

"Grandpa I already-"

"Alex, didn't your dad teach you not to interrupt? Just listen. Now because of this possibility I think I have some ideas."

"I can already turn into a raven!" I shouted, having had enough of him ignoring me.

"What? Nonsense. I mean...are you sure?"

"Umm, let me think. Yes! I've been trying to tell you that! I've been able to change for months now. I don't mean to brag, but I've gotten pretty good at it."

"Well then, this just goes even more into the ideas I already had been piecing together."

"And what are these ideas exactly?" Paul butted in, obviously wanting to get to the point already.

"Well...I don't think she's not going to die," he stated confidently. "If you've noticed, her body is slowly changing into something else. She is showing more and more signs of turning into one of them, but it is progressing very slowly. Normally this would happen quite fast. By now she would have either turned or died. I think the raven part of her is stopping both of those things. Whether or not it will stop the transformation entirely I am still not sure of. Most peculiar of all though is that, among the normal signs of changing such as her skin getting paler, she seems to be taking on some physical traits of the raven form. Yes, I see it quite clearly now. Just look at her hair, as we noticed before; it wasn't like that the other day when I saw her."

I took in each word silently, considering what he was telling me. My relief at being told I wasn't going to die was unexplainable—but I was still uncertain whether he was right or not. There was no way for any of us to be completely sure. Without warning, he stood from the table and came to my side. The roughness of his fingertips pressed delicately against my wrist.

"Hmm. Your heart rate is quite slow. I think the raven in you definitely won't let this kill you, but I'm afraid you may eventually turn completely into a vampire. As the process continues you will stop aging, you'll grow cold and numb; you'll even start to crave blood. Without it you would grow beyond exhausted, eventually dying without it." He moved his hands to my head, holding it still and gazing deep into my eyes as if looking intently for something. "Ah, yes. It is as I feared, I think. You are still turning; the raven in you can't fight it forever...it has only slowed the process. I stand by that we should just kill you now, before-"

"You watch your mouth. Dad or not, I won't sit here and let you talk about killing my daughter like that. She is your granddaughter for God's sake," Paul chimed in furiously, his hands balled into fists on top of the table.

"Well son, think about it. She will end up hungering for human blood. If she keeps any of the raven in her...just imagine how devastating she could be? You wouldn't kill her to save hundreds? Thousands? How many vampires do you know that have ever been able to completely stop their thirst for human life?"

"I know of at least one," I said quietly, before I had the opportunity to stop myself. This was probably not the best time to introduce Salem.

"What? You...*know*...a vampire?" Richard said with disgust.

"Yep ... well, two now," I mumbled, "but it isn't what you think. Salem can be trusted; he's harmless to us."

"Harmless?!" he shouted. "No vampire is *harmless*. I stand by what I said; we should be done with you and your friend. As soon as a person becomes a vampire, they are no longer themselves!"

"That's not entirely true," Paul said, to my surprise. "That vampire saved her life...more than once."

"Saved her life?" my grandfather asked, arching a gray eyebrow.

"You heard me. The last time... well... Alex had just been beaten up pretty badly by another vampire, a malicious one, and," I heard my father's voice crack, then he cleared his throat, "Salem had to turn her to save her life ... there was no other way. I...I let him do it."

"You encouraged this?!" Richard shook his head in disgust. "He didn't save her; he destroyed her! You let a vampire kill your daughter!"

"She's not dead."

"She might as well be! She'd be better off."

"I wanted this," I said angrily. "Salem asked before turning me. In the end, it was my choice. I chose to become a vampire."

"How could anyone want such a thing?!" he spat in response, leaving my side.

"She's in love with him," Paul said listlessly. I wondered if he was still uncomfortable with the relationship between Salem and me, but I didn't have to ask to know the answer.

"In love with a vampire?" Richard gawked at me as if I was some sort of abomination—which, I suppose in his eyes I was. I had become my own enemy. "This story just gets worse and worse, doesn't it? If I didn't know better I'd think I finally went mad! Maybe I'm up in my hospital room staring at walls."

"Let me put it to you this way," I heard a voice coming from the living room. The lights were out, and the curtains were drawn; all I could see was Salem's thin silhouette in the gentle glow from the windowsill. "Imagine Samantha, the love of your life, becoming a vampire. Before you begin insisting upon no longer loving her because she has become a 'monster', take into account that she is still the beloved woman you had always known—she doesn't feast on human blood, she is caring and generous, and she still loves you," he paused for a second and stepped into our view, "however, you are a mere mortal with a limited lifespan, you are nearing your final breath each and every day while she continues to be young and beautiful—would you not desire to be immortal with her, eternally together?"

Richard's eyes bore into Salem's, and I saw the quiver of his lips, the moisture in his eyes as he thought about my grandmother. He hung his head and sighed. "I want nothing more than to be with her forever...I'd give anything to have her back, even for a day."

"Exactly. So then, perhaps you can understand Alex's situation a little better."

"It still disgusts and befuddles me that a human could fall in love with a vampire." My grandfather slouched in the dining chair and looked up as Salem entered the room completely. "You're the one that turned her, then?"

"I am, and I regret it with every fiber of my being ... but at the same time, there is nothing more I could ever want in the world." He half-smiled. "The alternative was...well, I'd rather not think about it."

"You're quite unlike any vampire I've ever met," Richard commented when Salem took a seat at the table. "The next thing you'll try to tell me is that you don't drink blood, I suppose?"

"Not entirely. It is true that I have to have blood to live, just as you need food for your body. I get all the blood I need from animals...deer, rabbit, never humans. Even upon turning Alex, I did not consume the blood I extracted," Salem replied simply and explained to him how he had refused to hurt an innocent human.

"Unbelievable ... " the old man mumbled.

"I intend to make sure Alex is the same way. That is if what you think is true, and she does eventually turn completely. Do you really believe she will live through this, so to speak?"

"I do," Richard confirmed, never taking his eyes off of Salem. "And what about this second vampire? I guess I'm supposed to think she's all nice and innocent too?"

"That would be my half-sister, Hannah," Salem replied timidly. "She is sort of the cause of this whole ordeal."

"Hannah is the one that attacked me," I explained quietly.

"Nearly killed you is more like it!" Paul barked. "I don't see how you're letting her live after that."

"It was all a misunderstanding, dad … " It was hard to keep my voice straight, as part of me was still uncertain if we were making the right choice.

"I don't understand you, kid. You take all these risks, ruin your own life, and look at you. Bah! I'll give you the benefit of the doubt. But don't think that I won't kill the lot of you if it comes to it."

"You have nothing to worry about," said Salem. "I have never wanted anything more than animal blood, and I know Alex will be the same. My sister is already doing quite well, also."

"For someone that's been feasting on humans for…however long, I don't imagine she'll find it very easy to cope. You better watch her real close, and if I hear of her even licking someone's paper cut, I'll put her down myself," Richard warned.

"That shouldn't be a problem," a familiar melodic voice filled my ears. It didn't surprise me in the least that no one had heard her enter the house. "There is one more thing we need to discuss, though."

"Who is this?" Richard gasped, staring at the beautiful young woman who stood in the doorway.

"Don't freak out, but this is Hannah," I said, watching my grandfather cautiously. "What is it, Hannah?"

"The vampire you spotted on the way to Littlehaven … I saw her."

Hybrid

 Hannah informed the four of us that she had spotted the mysterious auburn-haired vampire lurking out in the woods, but unfortunately, her good streak of feasting on animals had become obsolete. The vampire had been seen crouching over a dead corpse of what Hannah said was a young child, and she fled from the scene before Hannah could get a better glimpse.

 "This isn't good," I groaned. "We need to go stop her before she kills anyone else."

 "Let's not get ahead of ourselves," Salem said thoughtfully. "Are you positive she was the one that killed the child?"

 "Without a doubt." Hannah frowned. "She was very obviously feasting on them at the time. I hate to admit it, but it was so difficult to ignore the smell of the fresh blood."

 Richard shot her a nasty glare. "And how do we know you didn't kill the girl and are just covering your tracks, eh?"

 "Grandpa! She wouldn't do that!" I said, surprising myself by defending her. "Besides, her eyes aren't red. If she had drunk human blood, they'd be basically glowing by now."

"If it is true that our new visitor out there has switched back to humans," Salem added, "then she must be stopped."

"Alexis should have no trouble hunting her, especially with her new powers," Richard replied, and now all eyes were set on me—including Hannah's, a look of envy.

Richard smirked at me. "You are no doubt going to be stronger and faster now. Plus, your senses are heightened. I am curious though…"

"Curious about what?" I gulped.

"I'm not sure exactly. It's just that, well … the raven part of you is affecting the vampire part of you in this form. I just wonder what, if anything, it will do to your bird form."

"Well, go on then, get with it," Hannah butted in bitterly.

"Wait, let's go outside first. I don't want to break anything if for some reason I can't control the form anymore."

I felt self-conscious as everyone surrounded me outside by the lake. The sky was darkening and I stared at the wide, luminous moon as it eased its way from behind the tall mountains. Averting my eyes, I focused my thoughts entirely on phasing. I blocked out everything else, including memories of Salem being in danger or hurt, as I knew now that merely concentrating on phasing would be enough to change.

I shut my eyes, picturing myself as the majestic ebony raven. Although accustomed to the twisting discomfort of my body changing shape, I didn't know what to expect this time. Would things be different in this form too?

I had felt nothing, but was somehow certain I had taken form. The familiar feeling of floating in the air was not there, however. I opened my eyes and looked down to see nothing but my same-old human body. Why hadn't I been able to change?

As I looked up at my four companions to tell them the bad news, I noticed they were all standing in shock. If Paul's mouth had been gaping open any further, it would have been on the ground.

"What's wrong?" I asked with a twinge of panic. "Why am I not changing?!"

"Well, I wouldn't quite say you aren't changing ... " Salem replied quietly and pointed toward the lake. "Have a look ... "

I obliged and approached the edge of the shore. The image reflected on the water made me scream. Falling to my knees, I glanced at the girl staring back at me and shook my head. This was all wrong. My hair was no different from this morning, but my eyes were piercing black orbs—the eyes of a raven. I glanced down at my hands and saw that my ordinarily short nails were long, fierce talons capable of shredding something—or someone—to pieces. My eyes focused on the reflection again, and I noted two massive, shimmering black wings protruding from my back. I quickly turned and looked at Salem, my eyes full of questions.

"What am I supposed to do like this?" I cried.

"Unfortunately, I think you will have to figure that out for yourself," he replied with a frown. "Maybe you should adjust to it, learn what you are now capable of, and get accustomed to this new form before you go hunting again."

"That's a wise idea," Richard added, stepping back some as he marveled at my appearance. I could tell that he was frightened, yet enticed at the same time.

"Do you think I will still be able to fly?" I could hardly bear to imagine not being able to feel the familiar sensation of flying over the world, being one with the wind.

"Well, try it and find out," Hannah said and gave me a surprising hopeful smile.

The wings expanded, and I willed them to move without even a single thought. My feet were hovering barely a foot over the earth in seconds, and I could hear the loud beating of wings behind me. A grin spread across my lips as a thought swept through my mind. Salem backed away slightly as I levitated toward him, but the reassuring smile I gave him made him stop. My deathly talons retracted as though claws of a wild cat, and I enveloped him in a tight embrace and within moments, we were hovering several feet above the lake.

"This is ... lovely," he said as he took in the surroundings. The water rippled beneath us, shimmering with each stroke of moonlight. Hannah, Richard and Paul gazed up at us in amazement as we grew ever higher. I stared deeply into Salem's eyes as we began twirling through the air, as if dancing on an invisible floor. He smiled at me, not an ounce of fear shown on his flawless face. Despite how he looked, his hands were clenched tightly onto my waist as though he was afraid I would drop him.

"Now you know how I feel every time you carry me upstairs." I laughed. The wind whipped around us, blowing my hair about.

"This will come in handy, Alex," Salem said as he continued to marvel at the land below from a height he had never before seen it from. "If ever you need to save someone, you can just whisk them up to safety and then carry on fighting."

"I guess you're right," I replied. "It's nice not being confined to that little bird body, but hopefully I'm never in that sort of situation."

"Hopefully," he agreed and smiled admirably at me. "In a way, I am thankful for what has become of you ... but I still can never forgive myself."

"You'll learn to forgive yourself, Salem. After all, you are stuck with me forever now. Plenty of time."

"That is all I could ever ask for."

"Me too," I replied and tenderly pressed my lips against his, then lowered us to the ground.

As our feet met the dew-covered grass, Hannah ran toward us with a wide smile. "Can I take a turn?" she asked pleadingly.

I laughed and pulled her into my arms. She felt thin and fragile, despite the strength I knew she possessed. "Just don't expect any kisses," I said as we rose from the ground.

"You can save all of that mushy crap for Salem." She made a disgusted expression, and then laughed as I spun us around above the lake. Despite her vast age, despite her past and what she had become, in this moment of laughter and giggles, I could see the same little girl from the vision of Salem's past, and knew we had made the right decision to let her live.

I lowered us to the water's surface and dipped our feet into the cool liquid as we skid across the rippling waters. Once we reached land, I released her and caught my breath. I was surprised I could already control my new strength and abilities so easily.

Everyone continued to stare at me as I stood at the water's edge, once more taking in the reflection that stared back at me. Salem approached my side and intertwined his hand with mine. I felt some relief at his touch, now admiring his figure next to mine on the water's surface.

"Do you still think I'm pretty, even like this?" I asked bashfully.

"I would consider you beautiful no matter what, Alexis," he replied and pulled me close. "Just as I know you would find me no less attractive had you met me and I was still covered head-to-toe in burns."

I smiled. "Nothing could make you less beautiful to me. From the very first day I met you, I knew there was something special about you."

The perfection of the moment was broken when an idea—a memory—dawned on me. Salem had told me that when Raziel turned him, he could see his past, present and bits of his future. What had Salem seen of me when he bit me? I was afraid to ask, afraid to know—even though I was almost certain I had no reason to be.

"Salem ... " I uttered. "There is something I need to ask you."

"Anything."

"What did you see-"

"We should head inside," Richard interrupted. "It's late and I don't know about any of you, but I'm tired and twice as hungry!"

I sighed and looked up at Salem. "I guess this can wait until later ... "

After dinner, it was decided that Paul would sleep on the sectional in the living room, and Richard could have the guest room. Hannah kept to herself downstairs while Salem and I retreated to our room. Before entering the house, I had changed shape and felt much more comfortable as my ordinary self—if I could even consider it ordinary any more.

It appeared that my hair would never be the same again, but I wasn't entirely upset about that. I found that I didn't feel an ounce of sleepiness yet and wondered how long it would take to get used to that once I had fully changed. I could do anything I wanted—within reason—and never lose a wink of time. I was overwhelmed with the fact that I finally had what I wanted. There was no longer the aching desire to become immortal, because I was slowly on my way there. Eternity with Salem was within my grasp!

Once we were both snuggled up on the black satin covers, I lay my head against Salem's chest and sighed heavily. I was afraid of the upcoming days. It wasn't just the idea of facing this new vampire, but also training myself to use this new form as a weapon—which didn't seem all too difficult—and the fact that sometime soon I would become fully undead. My heart would stop beating. The very idea was difficult to comprehend. How long was it going to take for me to adjust to the lack of the sound? How long would it take Salem to adjust to it? What concerned me more than that was the fact that I would grow a distaste for ordinary food. No matter how much I tried to convince myself, I knew I would never be comfortable killing innocent animals.

"What is on your mind?" Salem's pleasant voice was calm as it interrupted my thoughts, and he ran his fingers through my hair. "You seem tense."

"There is just so much going on," I replied and laughed dryly. "That's how things have been ever since I met you, though … so I guess I should be used to it by now."

"I am sorry if I have caused you any stress, Alex. But, as you have said yourself, things would be like this regardless if you had met me or not," he replied. "Well, maybe not entirely. You may still be fully human right now had I never become involved."

"That's not what is bothering me at all. It was more to do with hunting this vampire; I have a bad feeling about it, for some reason."

"I am sure you will do fine, and if things get out of hand I will be there in the shadows. Waiting."

"Thanks, but I'm still worried for some reason." I paused and sighed again. "There was also something I wanted to ask; I was just about to before we were interrupted earlier ... "

"I remember," he said and moved to where he could see my face. "You can always confide in me about anything."

"I know that ... it's just that not everything is so easy to talk about." I frowned and shuffled around nervously on the bed. "It's about something Raziel said."

He cringed at the mentioning of his Sire's name and then nodded knowingly. "You want to know what I saw when I bit you?"

"Yes," I whispered.

He smiled and stroked the side of my face. "Are you sure you wouldn't prefer to find out on your own, in time?"

I shook my head, "No, Salem ... I want to know now. I want to know everything, so I can be prepared for it."

"You would rather know now, and ruin any potentially pleasant surprises?" He frowned with uncertainty. "The future is something I have often contemplated during my many years upon this planet. While it is tempting and almost painful wondering what the future holds for you, in the end, I truly believe it is wisest to wait to see the outcome when the time is right. Besides, futures are not set as firmly in stone as the past."

Another sigh escaped my lips. It didn't seem there would be any persuading him tonight. "What about my past? Were there any glimpses of that?"

"Yes." He smiled—it was a joyful, affable smile. "I saw portions of your childhood. The bond between you, Karen and Jason is impressive ... beyond anything I ever shared with any friends. I witnessed the day Desmond deserted you. I never knew it hurt you so much. You became withdrawn and depressed for a long time. That was difficult to watch." His expression didn't falter despite the subject matter. "I saw the day we met, our first kiss, your unfortunate kiss with Jason and your reaction, fights between you and Paul. I saw the night you flew away from me, as well as the day you went to the cafe."

"Wow ... " I muttered. "I wish I could see inside your mind."

"There is nothing in there that you are missing out on."

"It would be interesting to be able to see what your life was like back when you were mortal," I said thoughtfully.

"Those memories were mostly all stripped from me. As much as it would be wonderful to witness some of them again...I think I am happier without them. I would like to focus more on my present than my past. The memories of those times are ancient now."

"No matter how old a memory is, it's still important. Memories make who we are."

"I suppose you are right," he replied, then held my face in his hands. With a playful smirk, he swept his cool lips across mine, and I returned the gesture. My heart raced—a feeling that would soon be forgotten—as he kissed me harder. The temptation was difficult to ignore as our kisses grew more passionate. I was unfamiliar with such intimacy, but I relished every second of it: the feel of his smooth lips as they traced across my cheek, down my neck and along my collarbone, the tender caress of his soft hands against my skin.

I felt an undeniable craving I had never experienced before—I wanted him in ways that I hadn't even contemplated until this point. His kisses suddenly ceased, and he stared at me apologetically. "You cannot believe how long I have waited for a moment like this, Alex..." he whispered soothingly, "however, I have made a promise to myself that I fully intend to keep."

My eyes curiously examined his face, noting the subtle hint of bashfulness in his expression. "What promise?"

"While it may be ordinary for people these days to commit such acts without a ring identifying each other as partners, I am more accustomed to the idea of marriage before...intercourse." He lowered his eyes for a moment. "I hope this does not affect your views of me."

I couldn't help but smile at his remark. "I think I can handle it," I replied. "It's not like I'm in any rush."

"I want you to understand that it is not because I do not *want* to, of course," he replied sheepishly.

"I know," I said with another smile and kissed him lightly. All I could think of now was the prospect of potentially marrying Salem someday—is that what he had been hinting at? Would I eventually become Mrs. Young? My heart fluttered at the idea. Salem ran his fingers gently through my hair and began humming a quiet, unfamiliar tune as I lay my head against his chest. The sound was relaxing and I let my eyelids fall shut, but knew that sleep would not come.

Practice

    The sun peeked in through the black curtains of the bedroom window, barely visible through the canopy over the bed. Most mornings, I would rush to the restroom to relieve myself, but today I found no need for it. Instead, I remained curled up beside Salem, who smiled warmly at me. I wish I had felt comfortable enough to smile at that moment, but my thoughts were occupied with worries again. My body was adapting more and more to becoming a complete vampire, and a huge part of me was terrified. Would I feel further pain upon the full transition, or would it be a smooth, hardly noticeable change? There was no one to ask, as no one knew the answer—I just had to wait and find out, and that made it harder than knowing what awaited me in the future. Maybe Salem knew the outcome through visions of my future, but he wasn't sharing.

    A knock sounded at the bedroom door and Salem hastily climbed off of the bed and went to the door to find Hannah peeking in at us. She had a wild grin on her face that made me curious if she somehow knew what Salem and I had talked about last night.

"Have a good night?" She smirked, scrunching her nose up a little in disgust as well.

"That is really none of your business, Hannah," Salem replied. "What do you want?"

"The humans are awake and want you two to come downstairs. They want Alex to start getting used to her new abilities as soon as possible, to hunt our little friend out in the woods; I suppose."

"We will be down in a moment," he said and shut the door as his half-sister walked away.

I got out of bed, changed into a clean pair of clothes and draped my arms around Salem. "I love you," I whispered as his arms wound around my waist.

"I love you too," he replied sweetly and kissed the top of my head, "more than you could ever know."

One brief kiss was shared before we reluctantly released each other and went downstairs. Paul and my grandfather were sitting at the dining room table again, both spooning cereal into their mouths. I was still unaccustomed to seeing food present in the house without Salem summoning it in mid-air by request, but it was still too early for Richard to discover that part of Salem. I wasn't sure how he would react to it, although judging from the life he led and the knowledge he had of vampires, it shouldn't be that much of a surprise.

"So what is the plan today?" Salem asked as we entered the kitchen.

"Paul and I both feel that Alex needs to dedicate as much time as possible to learning how to kill a vampire in her new form—which shouldn't be too hard judging by those claws I saw," Richard said after swallowing a mouthful of cereal.

"What I'm curious about is her caw ... " my dad added, putting his spoon down and staring thoughtfully in my direction. "That was awfully useful, hope you didn't lose it."

"I don't see any reason why she wouldn't still possess the ability. She is, after all, still a raven," Salem replied. "It might be difficult for her to figure out how to use it again, however."

I shrugged my shoulders. "I'll figure it out somehow."

"I hope so." Paul frowned. "Your aunt called about an hour ago saying there have been some bizarre stories spreading through the office. Lots of unsolved murders all over the country, people are saying it's almost a repeat of the 'Denver Slayings' only more brutal." I cringed at the memories as he spoke. "There've also been sightings of a strange woman hanging around in the cemetery, darting off into the woods when spotted, and most disturbingly—around my trailer park."

"Oh no. Has anyone in the park been hurt, or worse?" I asked.

"Not that I know of."

"That's good at least."

"I've been keeping watch around town while I'm out hunting, and I haven't seen her since the last time I told you. She almost seems to be looking for something—or someone," Hannah said. "She's acting really weird for a vampire. Most of us try to stay away from places where there would be lots of people at once, like the trailer park."

"That is weird," I mumbled, my worries about this vampire only growing stronger. There was something off about the whole situation. "Looks like I need to get ready as soon as possible." I looked from Salem to Hannah, then back again. "I need to try the caw, but I ... I need someone to use it on."

"I'll be your victim," Hannah volunteered. "It's only fair, after what I did to you."

I couldn't tell if the smile on her face was from wanting to help or from some sort of satisfaction in the memory of our fight—either way I wasn't about to disagree with her. "Well, I guess we should get to it, then." I sighed and headed out the back door.

The lake was sparkling under the influence of the sun's bright beams. It was a marvelous sight, but I had little time to enjoy it. I wasn't prepared for this at all. In my original raven form it was easy to figure out—open my mouth, make a noise, and the vampire crumbled to their knees at the piercing sound.

Hannah followed me out to the field where we had once sat on a blanket together. It seemed like so long ago now, and indeed much had happened since. I tried to ignore the contempt I felt toward her as I recalled all this recent history. She stood a few feet away from me, perfectly still. I had to admit that she was beautiful; Salem *wasn't* the only exception. The way her hair shimmered as the sunlight swept across it, it looked like strands of thin gold sprouting from her scalp and laying delicately across her shoulders.

My eyes lowered temporarily as I focused on transforming. The familiar rush of vibrant feathers surrounded me and spun through the air as a gush of wind blew passed us. I could feel the weight of the wings on my back, the growth of my nails, and I couldn't help but smirk as Hannah recoiled some at my appearance. I wondered how different I looked in the daytime.

"Just talking isn't going to work anymore," I said, somewhat to myself.

"Apparently not," Hannah answered, bracing herself for the impact of the sound I was potentially going to make ... assuming I ever figured it out. "Try making a cawing sound?" she suggested with a quiet giggle.

I did as she suggested, but that failed terribly. Hannah found some sort of delight in my failure and started laughing a little harder. I hoped now that I could figure this out soon, if for nothing else than to shut her up.

Inhaling deeply, I shut my eyes and pictured myself as an actual raven. Some things had been so much easier that way, but in a sense I was more comfortable in this form—I felt it would give me some advantages that the raven couldn't. I attempted to scream, but it did nothing but burn my throat. I thought over other alternatives, regardless how silly they seemed: whistling, yelling, imagining myself cawing, and then I shrieked as loud as my voice could manage. My lips curved into a wide smile as Hannah hunched over with her hands over her ears at the sound.

"I did it!" I exclaimed, jumping up and down. I felt like a complete fool, but I was proud of my accomplishment. Hannah stood up squinting from the aftereffects of the sound.

"Good. Now do it again," she insisted. "Practice makes perfect, right?"

"Right, of course." I nodded and let loose another shrill shriek that sent her tumbling over. Again and again we tried until she couldn't tolerate the sound any longer. Somehow it didn't affect my throat at all, unlike when I had simply yelled and screamed.

"Looks like you got that down pretty well. Now let's see you use those new nails of yours on me."

"What?! No!" I gasped. "I'm not going to hurt you."

"Oh come on Alex, we both know I deserve it. We need to know everything you are capable of, and what better way than by testing it on a vampire, right?"

I shook my head. "Couldn't I just go out hunting and find some random vampire to kill?"

"Right, that's a good idea." She rolled her eyes. "And what if it doesn't work, or you can't do it at all? Stop being a baby and just do it."

"Fine." I sighed in defeat and stared down at the long, sharp nails protruding from my fingertips.

"It might hurt for a little while, but you know I'll heal quickly," she said reassuringly. "I won't fight back this time, just to see what kind of damage you can do—then we'll have a real test."

It felt wrong attacking Hannah when she was standing defenseless before me, letting me lash out at her fragile pale skin. She winced with each swipe of my nails, but not a single scream escaped her tightly sealed lips. She was stronger than any vampire I had ever attacked before, but it was no surprise. Having been raised and trained by Raziel, there was no doubt in my mind that she was capable of terrible things—even worse than what she put me through.

"Stop," she finally said through clenched teeth. I pulled back, retracting my bloodied talons and eying the wounds I inflicted. Her arms were covered in long, thick gashes, and a few scratches marked her cheeks and neck, with some notably larger ones along her abdomen. As I stared, transfixed at the gory mess I had made, the cuts slowly began to stitch themselves together as if nothing had ever happened. Hannah's eyes were clamped shut tightly as she concentrated on her regeneration.

"I'm sorry. Was it too much?" I asked hoarsely.

She shook her head slowly. All evidence that she had ever been injured at all had vanished, aside from the blood staining her clothing. Before I was even given a second's thought, her eyes were open—bright red and menacing—and she tackled me to the ground.

My instincts kicked in instantly. I shoved Hannah off of me, kicking her hard in the side, but it barely fazed her. It felt strange not being a bird, but I adjusted to it quickly, relearning the proper fighting techniques Paul had taught me during my weeks of extensive training. As she prepared to pounce, I let loose a loud shrill that caused her to falter. With the use of my brilliant ebony wings, I hovered above the grassy field and soared toward Hannah. My claws were extracted and piercing her skin within seconds. It was difficult to stop myself; some part of me hungered to attack, ached to kill.

I shook my head and pulled back, retracted my claws and stared in disbelief at the crumpled body lying before me.

"H-Hannah?" I gasped, kneeling beside her and turning her over to look at me. To my surprise, she was smiling.

Her wounds once more began to fade, and she sat up. "You'll make a good vampire yet." She laughed, then grimaced at the torn fragments of her blood-stained lavender blouse.

I smiled apologetically at her clothing and helped her up from the ground. "So it is normal to have the sudden urge to rip your throat out?" I asked, feeling somewhat disgusted with myself.

"It isn't exactly normal to feel that way toward one of your own, but I think your Waldron instincts are mingling with your vampiric ones," she explained. "Which isn't really a bad thing, it could make you an even better hunter ... and I can't believe I am okay with this."

"It must be a real struggle for you, huh?" I asked quietly as I shifted back into my human form. "Salem means a lot to you, though. I can see it in your eyes. You don't want to betray his trust, otherwise you would probably be out there killing people at this very second—and my father and grandfather would be such easy victims to you right now."

She shrugged her shoulders and glanced back at the lake. "It hasn't been easy, but I'm doing okay. The smell of your relatives' blood is almost too much sometimes though, which is why I try to stay out of the house as much as possible ... just in case."

I thought for a moment, reflecting on the way Salem smelled in comparison to Hannah—her scent wasn't quite as foul as it used to be. The smell of burning wood was still pretty strong, though, and I wondered if it had anything to do with her near death experience in the burning house. That had been so long ago.

"You went back to the house, didn't you?" I asked as I studied her scent some more. There was a subtle hint of artificial vanilla still clinging onto her even though it had been days since she last applied the body spray.

"What are you talking about? I've been right here with you this entire time..."

"No. I mean...back to the house you were raised in. You went back after the fire, didn't you?"

"Oh...yes...I did," she confirmed. "Lots of times actually. The remains are long gone now, of course. I spent plenty of days there when I was still young and mortal, though." She sighed and looked toward the Victorian. "Their bodies were still there ... just bones among the piles of ash and burnt wood. We gave them a proper burial, Daniel and I. He took mother's death even worse than I did."

"His love for your mother was strong," I commented. "That is the one thing I admired about him."

She smiled at me. "It's nothing in comparison to the way Salem feels about you. I don't hate it as much as I did at first...now that you are technically one of us. It still stuns me that he could fall in love with a human to begin with though. I guess him being the way he is ... it isn't as impossible as I make it sound."

"If it weren't for Raz—Daniel—he never would have known about me ... "

"Well, maybe it was all meant to be this way, and the two of you were destined to meet." She laughed.
"Twin souls," I whispered quietly to myself and smiled as we set off for the house.

Scents

What occurred outside did not need retold, as apparently everyone was watching through the window behind the sofa. Everyone was impressed, although Salem appeared a little forlorn as he watched Hannah and me make our entrance. I eyed him curiously, but his expression altered to a simple smile almost instantly. Richard and Paul were unsurprisingly ecstatic and impressed. Both felt that I was on the verge of being prepared to encounter the mysterious woman lurking around Willowshire. I had little time to waste; every minute of preparation meant another moment she could be taking an innocent life.

"Dad?" I said as a painful thought struck me hard. "Kim knows the name of everyone that's been injured or murdered by this vampire, right?"

"Your friends are fine," he said with a reassuring smile. "She's been keeping a close eye on them from a distance, by my request."

With a sigh of relief, I relaxed a little and turned to look at Salem. "Can we talk for a minute? Alone?" I asked quickly, and directed him upstairs. I sat on the edge of the mattress and gestured for him to sit beside me. "You seem a little tense, Salem."

"I'm fine," he replied with a very obvious false smile.

"You didn't like watching that," I stated.

"No, I didn't," he admitted, staring down at his hands. "I knew everything would turn out fine, but I am sure you would have felt the same."

"Right ... "

"What did you need to talk to me about?"

"I noticed as soon as I was conscious, after you turned me ... that you have a very distinct smell," I said cautiously, "then, I noticed the same with Hannah. Is this normal?"

He smiled at me for a moment, and then nodded. "Upon becoming a vampire, your senses heightened. You will find you can hear and smell things that no mere mortal ever could, and your vision could match that of a hawk. If you get close enough to someone, you will find that you are able to distinguish specific scents that apply to that person," he explained. "Take Paul for example. He works in an auto shop; therefore you will often find that he smells strongly of oil—even after days of being away from the shop. It's practically become a part of who he is, ingrained deeper than the pores of his skin."

"That's why Hannah smells so much like burnt wood, then ... because of how often she visited the old house?"

"Precisely."

"And why do you smell like water and chamomile?"

He arched a brow. "No one has ever told me what I smell like." His laughter was light and his eyes distant. "My mother often had me brew chamomile tea to aid her in sleeping...it is amazing how much the sense of smell links us to fond memories."

"And water?"

"Perhaps because I live so close to a lake." Salem shrugged.

"There is one other scent that seems to have attached itself to you, but I can't quite put my finger on what it is."

"What does it remind you of?"

I looked down and my cheeks reddened somewhat. "It sort of reminds me of old paper."

"Ah." Salem smiled and lifted my head up. "I read a lot of old books, remember? Before we met I must have read a book or more a day. One gets bored at night when they no longer need sleep."

"Of course!" I laughed. "That makes a lot of sense. Hannah also kind of smells like metal, or rust."

"My guess is that after wearing the same locket for countless years, the scent of the metal has latched itself to her."

"Oh," I replied, and then glanced up into his eyes. "What do I smell like to you, Salem?"

Salem looked at me with a gentle smile, and replied with a simple answer—"Ivory."

A knock sounded at the door. Immediately, the scent of oil caught my attention. It was odd how I never really noticed it before, but now that Salem mentioned it—it was intense.

"Come on in, dad," I said and watched the door swing open, revealing Paul's shocked face.

"How did you know it was me?"

"I could smell you," I replied. "You might not realize it—but you smell very strongly of oil."

He nodded. "Makes sense. You must be coming closer and closer to being changed completely ... "

"Does that concern you?" Salem asked.

"Why wouldn't it?" Paul replied crossly. "My daughter, who I've spent years trying to protect from vampires, is becoming one of them!"

"Just calm down," I said sharply. "You agreed to let it happen—it was either this or death."

"I know." He frowned. "I just wish it hadn't come to this. It isn't as easy for me as I have been trying to make it seem."

"I understand ... it hasn't been easy for me, either ... " It was a lot harder than he, or even Salem, were aware. "So...what did you want?"

"I'm going home for a little while," he replied cautiously. I leapt up from the edge of the bed.

"You can't go back there!" I exclaimed. "It's not safe!"

"I'll be fine, Alex," Paul replied with a laugh. "Did you forget that I'm a hunter too? I hope she does come poking around the park again."

"This isn't just a regular old vampire ... there's something different about her. I have this bad feeling, you know?"

"Ah, come on now, I'll be fine. Besides, I need to get some things to take over to the auto shop. The store's been closed for too long with me hanging out over here, got to make a living you know. Vampire huntin' doesn't pay the bills, and not all of us have a little Salem summoning us everything we need."

"I'm sorry, dad ... I can't help but worry. Maybe Hannah should go with you, just in case."

Paul burst out in sudden laughter. "I'm not taking that crazy bitch with me. She's probably more likely to kill me than the other one. Pardon the French, but seriously."

"Do not talk about her like that! She has changed," Salem glowered.

"Whatever dad, just go ... call if anything unusual happens."

"I will. You do the same." He turned to leave, and then glanced back at me. "Love ya, kid."

"Love you too, dad ... " I said quietly and followed him out of the room.

As I watched my father exit through the wide, white doors, I felt an aching uneasiness well up within me. Part of me longed to chase after him, force him to stay and keep him safe—but it wasn't my decision to make. He was a grown man, with a hand crossbow and the instincts of a hunter—he could take care of himself if anything happened ... right? No. I was foolish to let him leave! He had the weakest aim of any Waldron in the history of our ancestors! But it was too late. He was gone and out of sight. I heard the roar of the Wrangler's engine and the tires rolling across the gravel.

"He will be fine, Alex," Salem said quietly from behind me, resting an assuring hand on my shoulder. "If anything happens, we will know."

"How will we know?"

"He'll call us, like he said ... or Kim will." He didn't seem so sure; I could hear it in his voice—but for now, it was enough to convince me to relax—a little at least.

Richard entered the room, which was a good distraction for the time being. He wobbled into the kitchen with one hand against each wall or piece of furniture he came across in order to steady himself. I had never seen him appear so fragile, and it became clear to me just how old he was. Age had become less meaningful to me since I met Salem—especially since I became a vampire—and I hadn't taken the time to realize that my grandfather was well into his sixties or early seventies and didn't have many years left on this planet.

"Do you need help, grandpa?" I asked as I pulled myself away from the bothersome thoughts.

"It's all right, Alex," he said with a smile that produced a row of wrinkles at the corners of his mouth. "I forgot to bring my cane with me, and I am not used to walking down so many stairs."

"Salem ... could you?"

"What? Oh...yes, of course." He nodded, and I watched his eyes flicker for a brief second. An elegant, glossy cherry wood cane appeared in his hand. He passed it over to me, and I offered it to Richard, who stared at Salem with his mouth wide and gaping.

"Did-did he just ... " he froze mid-sentence and blinked his eyes really hard. "This boy is more than just a vampire?"

"Yes," I said quietly. "He's actually a relative to the very first woman burned at the stake for practicing witchcraft ... "

Richard shook his head and hesitated to take the cane. "Is this some sort of magic trick? Or a joke?"

"It is no trick, Richard," Salem said calmly. "If you can believe in the undead, surely you can come to realize that other unexplainable things are possible."

"There are no coincidences," I spoke quietly, recalling what Salem told me when I was just as doubtful as my grandfather. "It took me a while to believe it and accept it, but you'll get used to it."

Finally, the old man reached out and grasped the smooth wooden cane and limped over to us. He examined Salem closely, and to my surprise, he smiled widely. "I knew there had to be more to this world. I've always been a believer, deep down ... but after so many years without evidence, I began to lose hope."

"It isn't very common...well...not that I am aware of, anyway," Salem explained. "Hannah has an ability of her own as well."

"Does she?" Richard asked curiously. "Same as you no doubt? I mean you are siblings after all so it only makes sense that-"

"Half-siblings, actually. No, Hannah doesn't share the same gift as I do. She has the ability to minds and manipulate dreams."

"So, she can hear my thoughts, then?"

"Only if I touch you directly, so watch out," Hannah said slyly as she entered the room, waving her hands around and making ghost sounds.

"You stay away from me," Richard sat and glared. "I still don't trust you one bit, mind reader or not."

"You trust Salem, and you trust Alexis ... what's so different about me, old man?"

"You tried to kill my granddaughter!"

"And how many of my kin have you killed, huh? We're just following the way God made us. He made you to feast on animal flesh, plants, berries...he made us to feed on blood."

"God made you? Bah, Satan more likely."

"Grandpa!" I interrupted. "Just cut it out. You really need to give her a chance."

Hannah directed a thankful smile toward me. "Besides, if I was going to kill you...I would have done it already. Probably old and chewy anyway, yuck." She giggled wildly.

"Hannah! You cut it out too! How do you expect for them to trust you when you say crap like that?" I scorned.

"Oh come on, I was just having a bit of fun."

Richard huffed and took a seat at the dining room table. "I'll try...no promises though. Now, would someone be so kind as to make me some tea?"

"Any preference?" Salem asked.

"Earl Gray, if you have it. If not, then just whatever you have will do."

Salem, Hannah and I laughed as Richard stared with one shaggy gray eyebrow raised in our direction. Salem's pale blue eyes flashed violet yet again and a cup of steaming hot tea materialized on the table. "Enjoy," he said with a wink, grabbed my hand and led me out of the room.

"Where are we going?" I asked as I was tugged along beside Salem into the clearing. The smell of fresh flowers caught my attention, as well as the wood of the surrounding cedar trees. A hint of honey, perhaps from a nearby bee's nest, and then a wisp of something unpleasant yet delicious even so—blood. I sighed and looked toward the ebony-haired vampire. "We are hunting, aren't we?"

"Yes," he replied. "While I may be able to prevent myself from feeding frequently, you are still adapting to becoming a vampire and will need blood to sustain you. After a while, you might be able to ignore the cravings and maintain your strength without it, but if you intend to fight a vampire any time soon you are going to need to fill up. I am almost certain that is what was causing your exhaustion spells on the trip. Whether you like it or not Alex, you are going to need blood."

I groaned. "Couldn't I just have a hamburger or something?" Ordinarily, that would have sounded delicious—yet I felt no craving whatsoever.

"Listen, Alex," he said, and I did, expecting him to continue, but he didn't open his mouth. The forest was silent besides the occasional chirp of a bird and rustling of leaves—that's when I realized my heart had stopped beating.

"Does this mean it is final?" I gasped, reaching a hand to my chest and resting it against my heart.

"You are officially dead or undead, I guess … " he answered remorsefully.

"Why didn't I feel anything? Shouldn't I have noticed?"

"I think you felt all the pain of transformation directly after I turned you, even though the actual change happened gradually," Salem explained, taking my hand into his. "Are you scared?"

"No … " Maybe I was; I wasn't entirely sure. My feelings were jumbled and confused. I should be scared, yet somehow I felt relieved. "Not exactly. I feel a sense of relief now that it's all over."

He smiled somewhat, although I knew he wasn't completely happy—this wasn't at all what he had wanted. "There's an elk lurking to the east."

"Oh boy … " I mumbled with distaste, turning my head in the proper direction and taking a whiff of the air. The smell of the animal was intense and the urge I suddenly felt to kill it was overwhelming. Leaving Salem behind, I rushed toward the elk.

The creature was lapping at a small puddle of murky water, unaware of my presence as I watched stealthily from behind a tree. My feet moved quickly as I came closer to my prey, but I made no noise at all. I hunched over in a crouching position, mere feet from the elk and leapt onto it. The kick of the animal's hooves against my ribcage didn't hurt, but it was hard enough to knock me back. The elk turned toward me and snorted. It was far larger than I had expected. As I stared into its eyes, I could hear its heart racing. Unlike the rabbits, or deer...I knew this one wasn't going to simply try to run away.

Before I had time to think, it charged at me. Within a fraction of a second, I felt the horns pierce into my abdomen. The impact had doubled me over, and my arms lay across the creature's neck. The vampire instinct inside of me kicked in, and without thinking I snapped its neck with my arms. The elk fell over in a lifeless heap, and the heartbeat that had sounded so loud just moments before slowly ceased.

My fangs inched out from below my front lip, and I sunk them deep into the beast's throat. The rush of fluid filled me with an unfamiliar joy as it sated my thirst, and I didn't stop despite feeling full. The want—the need—was overpowering. I grasped the dead elk tightly in my hands as I quenched my thirst until a noise suddenly distracted me.

I shook my head and dropped the poor animal. Gasping in shock, I backed away. My hands were dripping with fresh, bright blood, and I immediately dunk them in the small puddle of water. The sound came again. It was somewhat of a faint, musical jingle.

My phone!

I reached inside my pocket and plucked out the small black cell phone. Jason's name appeared on the screen. With hesitation, I pushed the talk button and said, "Hello?"

"Alex!" he exclaimed. "How are you?"

"I'm ... good. I think," I mumbled, averting my eyes from the gory scene. There was blood soaking my pants and shirt, and I shuddered with disgust.

"Where are you?"

"I'm out ... " I replied, "With Salem. Do you need something?"

"I kind of wanted to introduce you to someone," he said somewhat oddly.

"Who?" Could it possibly be the auburn-haired vampire? Was she after Jason?

"Her name is Eila," he said with obvious enthusiasm. "I met her at Howard's last week."

"That's a...unique name," I replied, wondering what this could all possibly mean. I had to meet her, at least to know if she was the vampire or not. "When did you have in mind?"

"Anytime you're available. She'll be over in about an hour."

"Okay, I'll stop by then."

"Great! I can't wait!"

"Me either," I said and hung up. I nearly jumped when I discovered Salem standing behind me.

"Jason?"

"Yeah," I replied quietly. "He wants me to stop by the house later to meet some friend of his."

"May I join you?"

"I don't see why not."

"Alex, your stomach!" He finally noticed the wound from the elk.

"It's okay...I think. Well...it doesn't hurt at least."

"That's good, but you need to heal."

"Heal? I thought that sort of, just happened. On its own..."

"It can, but it takes far longer that way. To heal as quickly as you see me or Hannah heal, you must concentrate on it."

"Umm, okay...and how exactly do I do that?"

"To be honest I have not really thought about it in a long time. I am so used to it that I just do it naturally. Just try to relax, concentrate on the area that is damaged, and see it as well again inside your mind."

"Sounds easy enough…" I closed my eyes and thought of the tears along my abdomen. I saw how it was now, I saw the scene of what caused it, and I pictured it well again. I opened my eyes and looked down, expecting it to have worked. Instead, I saw the same gruesome mess as before. "Salem, why isn't it working?!"

"You have to relax, Alex. Just like when you were shifting from bird to human, you have to put yourself at peace."

I tried again. I put the focus in my mind on the healing itself, but felt nothing. I had to find something more fitting to calm me, so that it would work. Maybe it was because I missed him, or maybe because I had just talked to him … whatever the reason—I thought of Jason, and the healing came.

Lila

The house appeared as clean as last time from the outside. I still felt strange seeing the house where I had lived for so long. I could picture Janet's van parked perfectly in the driveway, where instead I found two cars—one of which was Jason's, the other I did not recognize. Salem and I exited the Alero and approached the front door. I knocked, although I knew they wouldn't have minded if I had just walked in...considering the place was technically mine.

"We're just here to make sure she isn't the vampire, and then we can go," I whispered to Salem as we waited for someone to answer.

The door opened slowly to reveal Mitch, who appeared a little apprehensive. "Hey, Alex," he said. "This is Salem?"

Salem nodded. "I am."

"Wow, Alex. Karen didn't mention he had an accent. Where's he from?"

"Wales," I commented, trying to peek over Mitch's shoulder to see inside the house. "Is Jason here?"

"Yeah, but he's kind of occupied at the moment," he answered awkwardly.

I arched a brow and gently pushed him aside. The kitchen was surprisingly clean and tidy. Not a single dish sat in the sink, the garbage can was empty, and the floor was swept. As I turned toward the living room, I gasped and looked away. Jason was sitting on my old loveseat, cradling some unfamiliar girl in his arms, their lips latched onto each other as if they were stapled together. Why did I feel a twinge of jealousy at this image? I didn't have feelings for Jason beyond friendship. Was it because now he would no longer be fawning over me? Shouldn't I think that was a good thing?

"Excuse us." Salem coughed suddenly, and I slowly turned back to look at the pair on the love seat. They were sitting upright, separated from each other and looking somewhat abashed. Now that she wasn't tangled up in Jason's arms, I got a good look at the girl beside him. She had a slightly rounded face, with perky red lips and almond-shaped brown eyes. A flowing mane of wavy brunette hair with vibrant honey highlights settled against her shoulders, and she didn't look up at us. She wore a pale yellow sundress that perfectly contrasted to her hair. At least I had my answer—this was, in fact, not the vampire I was after. She wasn't a vampire at all. She smelled heavily of metal and sunflowers, which led me to wonder what brought on those particular scents.

"Hey Jason ... " I said hoarsely, trying to find my voice. "Sorry ... you told me to come over whenever."

"Yeah, I'm sorry," he said and stood up from the couch. "This is Eila."

"I gathered that," I replied, and entered the living room. The atmosphere was definitely awkward and uncomfortable. Salem hovered behind me, observing the scene from afar.

"I think I know you," Eila said in a hushed voice. "You were in my music class!"

This didn't make any sense. Jason was with a girl from music class? Maybe it was just an elective she chose to get it out of the way. "You were in music class?"

"She plays the flute," Jason replied for her. "She is really good at it, too!" That explained the metallic scent, I guessed.

I shook my head in confusion. "This is coming from the boy who throughout middle and high school teased everyone for being in music class—including me!" I nearly shouted.

Jason hung his head in shame. "I know ... Eila scolds me for it enough, I don't need to hear it from you. I've matured since then, really. I understand that just because you are interested in music that doesn't make you a nerd."

"That's good to know, at least," I grumbled. "Was there any particular reason why you wanted me to come over here?"

"I thought you two might get along—considering you both like music and all," he said with a shrug. "And I thought Salem might be more comfortable with you coming over sometime if he knew I wasn't going to try anything."

"That is something that I hope never crossed your mind before," Salem growled from behind me.

"I can't promise I never thought about it," Jason replied and Eila stood and slapped him on the shoulder. "Hey, I'm sorry! I used to have a huge crush on Alex, but I promise you all of those feelings are gone. She's just a friend. Just like Karen."

What had this girl done to catch Jason's attention, and why did it bother me so much? She seemed friendly, if not a bit shy, and she was attractive ... but what did they have in common? Then again, what did Jason and I have in common? I guess that was irrelevant.

"You two met at Howard's, you said?" I said, ending the silence.

"Yes," Eila replied with a smile. "It's not the most romantic 'How did you two meet?' story, but it doesn't have to be. I was short a few cents and Jason told me not to worry about it, he would pay the extra. It was embarrassing at first."

"Then I asked her out to eat, and things went from there."

"How long has this been going on?"

"A couple of weeks."

"You two seem happy," I said, wishing I could leave now that I knew she wasn't any threat to my friends.

"Oh, we are!" Eila chimed in and grasped Jason's hand tightly.

I looked around the house, hoping to catch a glimpse of Mitchell hanging around somewhere. "Where'd your brother run off to?" I asked when I couldn't find him and didn't hear anything upstairs.

"He's probably outside in his new car. He barely leaves that thing."

"I'm going to go talk to him, if you don't mind." My question was directed at both Jason and Salem.

"Go ahead," Jason said.

"I will wait here," Salem replied, staring at Jason with distaste.

I headed out the front door. The lights were bright and shining almost directly in my eyes; however, it didn't bother me to look straight into them. I could hear music roaring from the radio, smell the gasoline and oil from within the car. The vehicle was bright-red and slick, much more appealing than my dull Alero. It was even more attractive than Jason's metallic blue PT Cruiser. I tapped gently on the driver-side window, but he didn't roll it down. As I prepared to knock again, I heard the doors unlock and walked to the passenger side and climbed in. The gray leather seat was comfortable and in just the right position to give me the perfect amount of leg room. My ears were overly sensitive to the sound blaring from the radio, so I covered my ears.

"Sorry," Mitchell said as he turned off the stereo. "What are you doing out here?"

"I came to talk," I replied.

He looked tense, tired and disheveled. Something was obviously bothering him.

"What about?"

"Well, first I wanted to congratulate you on the car!" I said and smiled. "I'm proud of you for keeping up with those hours for so long. I'm pretty sure I would've given up after day two."

I was relieved to see his lips curve upward in a small, amused grin. "It was well worth it."

"What kind of car is it?"

"It's a Mustang GT," he replied. "I saved a lot to afford this baby!"

"Is that why you spend so much time out here?" I asked, my voice growing a little more serious.

"Mostly ... "

"It's something to do with Eila, isn't it?"

He sighed. "It isn't that I don't like her. She's really sweet and treats Jason like a king—not to mention she keeps the place clean—but it feels weird being around him now. They're always together ... I am wondering if I should just find a place of my own or something."

"Oh, Mitchell ... " I frowned and pulled him into a comforting hug. "Don't say that. They're a brand-new couple. Things will settle down eventually, and it'll be back to the way things used to be, just with one extra body. I'm sure you'll get used to it."

"Maybe," he replied stubbornly as our hug ended. "It was nice when it was just the two of us ... but I guess that's how it works."

"Imagine if it were the other way around. You wouldn't want Jason stuck outside all the time, hiding away from you and your girlfriend."

"No, but I doubt that would even cross my mind," he said with a grin.

"See? It's all new to him, too."

"And what do you think about it, Alex?"

"Me?" I blinked. "Why would I care?"

"Because for the past sixteen years Jason had feelings for you, and then some new girl shows up, and he is suddenly head-over-heels in love with her. He says he doesn't feel anything for you anymore other than being a friend. Doesn't that make you even a little upset?"

I shrugged, although he was right. "A little ... but it's not a big deal. I'll get used to it too. It's better this way." I smiled, comforting myself with my own words.

"I guess you're probably right," he agreed and smiled at me. "Thanks for coming out here."

"Pft, you don't have to thank me. We're friends too you know. I've missed you both so much."

"We've missed you, too. You know you can come over any time. I'm not on the graveyard shift anymore, so I'm less of a zombie," he said with a chuckle.

He was less of a zombie, and I was closer to being one than I ever imagined possible. I wondered if this was something I would someday be able to confide in the Banner brothers about, or even Karen.

"I'll keep that in mind," I said. "I should probably head back now though."

"Are you sure? You could stay for dinner."

He seemed eager for company, but I knew I couldn't stay. "I'd love to, but I really can't. My grandpa is visiting, and I need to get back home to check on him."

"Your grandpa? I didn't even know you had any alive."

"Me either until a few weeks ago," I said. "Now he practically lives with me. So trust me when I say I know how it feels to have your house invaded."

We both shared a brief understanding smile, hugged again, and I left the car. After a quick farewell to Jason and Eila, Salem and I headed back home.

As we were driving back to the Victorian, my phone went off. Salem picked it up and hesitantly answered. A panicked expression slowly developed on his pale face as he listened to the voice on the other end.

"We need to turn around," he whispered, still listening intently to the person on the other line.

"What? Why?" I nearly shouted.

"Just turn around, Alex." His voice remained just as quiet and then he hung up the phone. "It's Paul."

Trailer Sixteen

"What? What is going on?!" I nearly veered off the side of the road as I yelled at Salem.

"Your phone said it was Paul, but a woman answered. She told me to go to trailer 16, bring no weapons, and don't act suspiciously," Salem said calmly, which I was certain was only in the hopes of getting me to relax.

"It's the vampire. It has to be. She has Paul. She's going to kill him!"

"We don't know that Alex. Maybe she just wants to talk to us."

"That's very likely, Salem!" I shouted. "How often do murderous, crazed vampires want to 'just talk'?!"

"Most likely never, but you need to calm down unless you want to crash and possibly kill someone!"

I turned the steering wheel quickly to the left as I almost rammed straight into the side of a van beside us. With a deep breath, I managed to relax somewhat, although inhaling practically did nothing for me—it was out of habit.

"Now, let's get to Paul's house...carefully," Salem said once I was more relaxed.

I nodded slowly, pulled into a vacant lot and turned the car around to head toward the direction of the trailer park. I began to wonder how my heart was not racing with fear as I sped along the road, and then it occurred to me that it was impossible. I didn't entirely miss the feeling of an anxious heartbeat. The sky was darkening overhead yet I could see just as clearly as if it was daylight.

"Bring no weapons," I mused. "Little does she know, I am a weapon. I bet she won't be expecting that."

"That's true. But do not act immediately. Wait until we know for certain she is our suspect, and at least give her a chance to explain herself."

"Why should I give her a chance to explain herself? She has been going around town killing people! For all we know Paul could be next!" I jerked the car into the trailer park and drove through the thin space until I reached the familiar peach-colored mobile home. Leaving my crossbow in the car, I climbed out swiftly and slammed the door shut. Salem followed me up the stairs to the thin, flimsy door. It was cracked open, and I could see a faint yellow glow emanating from within.

"Dad?" I called as I pushed the door open. "Are you here?"

No one answered. I stepped into the cramped place, discovering it was more of a mess than when I last visited. There were papers strewn across the floor, and what appeared to be old photographs. Ignoring the temptation was hard; I knelt down and picked up the nearest picture.

"Oh!" I gasped, nearly dropping the photo.

Depicted in the small square was an infant with very short brunette hair and hazel eyes. She was cradled in the arms of an auburn haired woman who stood next to a much younger version of my father; they were both smiling. I turned the picture over and glanced at a small inscription on the back:

Destiny, Paul and Alexis (1995)

Salem stared at the words along with me, no doubt coming to the same conclusion. This couldn't be real. It must have been some sort of mistake ... there had to be another explanation! I reached for the next closest thing, which turned out to be an old note.

'Dear Paul, August, 10, 1994

I can hardly believe we are about to be parents. I am so thrilled! I know it will be tough raising her, knowing ... what you are ... but we will make it through somehow. You must make me one promise, however—never, ever let Alexis know about your 'side job'. Let her live a normal life. We can protect her from it together. I know we can. Keep this note as a reminder. Just in case.

I love you so much, and I can't wait to hold our baby!
Love always,
Destiny'

I let the paper slip out of my hand.

"My mother ... " I choked out. "She's the vampire ... "

"You don't know that for certain, Alex. It could be a coin-"

"Don't you dare say 'coincidence'!" I shouted. "You are the one who told me there are none! This is happening! This is real!"

"Let's find your father and make sure he is safe," Salem replied quietly, averting his eyes for a moment.

I carefully edged down the hallway leading to Paul's bedroom. I had never gone this far into the trailer before, so initially I made the mistake of opening the bathroom door and a spare room. My eyes were fixated on the furnishing of the extra bedroom: a sleek white crib in the far corner of the room with a mobile with white lambs dangling overhead, a quaint dresser beside it in the same color, and a tan glider chair in the other corner beside a small window. I cautiously entered the room, my curiosity getting the best of me. How had Paul not shown this to me after all this time?

Lying inside the crib was a small, dusty, brown bear with a red bow-tie around its throat. I picked it up, rubbing the soft material gently when I felt something prick my finger. A tag dangled from the stuffed animal's left paw. I turned it toward me and read it:

To Alexis, from mommy

I dropped the bear into the crib and stepped away. This was all too much. Salem came up to me with intent to comfort me, but I pushed him away.

"Not now ... I need to get out of here ... We need to find Paul."

He nodded with a subtle frown and followed me out of the unsettling room. There was only one more door; it had to be Paul's room. I shut my eyes momentarily as I eased my fingers around the doorknob.

"Welcome, Alexis," an unfamiliar voice met my ears as I inched the door open. "I've been waiting for so long to see you again."

I gulped and forced the door the rest of the way open, finding the auburn-haired vampire sitting in the center of Paul's queen-sized bed with her legs crossed underneath her. The only other piece of furniture present within the room was a dresser, and atop it I noted something that might come in handy—one of Paul's crossbows. How had she missed it? I avoided looking at it for too long, in case she caught on.

My father was nowhere to be seen. It was remarkable how much she reminded me of myself. Her eyes were the same hazel; the shape of her face was almost a mirror image of my own.

"Come now, don't be shy," she said with an alluring smile. "Come say hello to mommy."

"You aren't my mother," I blurted out. "She was killed by a vampire eighteen years ago!"

"Ha!" Her laugh was light and sarcastic. "Had your father made even the slightest attempt to find me, maybe he would have managed to save me. But ... he never did. He just assumed I was dead."

"What? No, he said he saw...he said..." I wracked my brain trying to recall if my dad had said for certain he saw Destiny get killed. He had only said she was taken from him. "What really happened?" I asked, cautiously entering the room with Salem directly behind me.

"It wasn't the vampire's intention to turn me. He was in search of a Waldron, and mistook me as the hunter!" She laughed and shook her head. "You see, his grand plan was to turn a great vampire hunter into a weapon. He wanted to use them to take over families of other vampires and rule them—but when he found that I was only a mere ordinary human, he was furious. He called me weak and useless and offered to sell me as a slave to any other vampire who would take me."

"A slave?" I asked, wondering just what she had been put through.

"He would have kept me himself to do his bidding, but he had his hands full with some child. We traveled as far as Transylvania—how typical, right!" She burst into a fit of laughter, then resumed her story. "A man named Malik was instantly interested and Raziel bartered with him at a fair price."

"What could a vampire possibly trade for you?"

"Vampires need money too, Alex! How do you think they travel or afford homes?"

"How did you find your way back here ... ?"

She smirked, and her eyes appeared glossed over. "Come sit with mommy, and she will tell you the whole story."

"You can tell me from where you are."

"No, I need you closer, Alex ... please ... after all of these years, you must understand how much I need to touch you, to hold you."

With little hesitation, I stepped closer to the bed. Salem was right at my heels with each step until I sat beside the woman. She smiled pleasantly, almost fooling me into believing she was sane and friendly.

She brushed a snow-white hand across my cheek and smiled admiringly at me. "You have grown so much ... " Before I had the chance to respond, she gripped my hand tightly. "Malik taught me at least one useful trick," she said darkly, then swiftly turned my head to face her and look into her eyes.

It was all too familiar. Her eyes became pools of darkness, and then slowly images began appearing within her pupils. I felt myself being dragged in, pulled away from reality and into whatever vision she wanted me to see.

Suddenly I was standing in a courtyard. There was an elegant fountain in the center of the courtyard; however it was not filled with water. Blood trickled down from two holes in the throat of a statue depicting a horrified young child, and filled the pool at the bottom. I shuddered in disgust, and then a sound caught my attention and distracted me from the astonishing sight. To the left of the fountain was a woman hunched over the side of a cement bench. Her bare back was exposed through tears in the thin blue blouse she wore. Footsteps came from behind me, and soon a tall, slender man was in sight. He wore a cloak made of burgundy velvet over a white collared shirt—he appeared almost to be royalty. The hair atop his head was short and black, and he wore a devious smile as he approached the woman. He walked with his arms crossed behind his back.

"I hear that you have been misbehaving again, Destiny." His voice was soft, yet I detected a hint of malice behind it.

"I haven't done anything wrong!" she cried. "Please, let me go! I'll get back to work. I'll do better...I promise!"

"Ah, but what would be the joy in that?" He laughed darkly. "You know the rules. You disobey Lord Malik, and you are punished for it."

"Tell me, then—what have I done wrong?!"

"Guardsmen overheard you discussing your past with another slave. That is not allowed. You are not to speak to the other slaves, especially not on such topics. There is no friendship here, so don't go seeking it. You are to do whatever job is assigned to you and nothing more. No conversations with anyone beyond myself or a guard. You have no past. You have no future. Understood?"

"Yes, sir," she whimpered.

"Then let this be a reminder for next time." I watched as Malik unveiled a thick black whip from behind his back. Destiny wailed as the whip lashed at her skin three times, leaving large red gashes.

He laid the whip against the bench and offered a hand to Destiny. She reached out with intent to slap it then shut her eyes, inhaled and took it. I watched with confusion as he leaned toward her and kissed her delicately on the lips.

"You will forgive me, won't you?" he whispered into her ear. "We all have rules we must follow, no?"

She didn't reply, but he didn't appear to expect an answer.

Now I was following behind my mother as she stalked quietly through a crowded city. It was dark and scarcely anyone was seen walking along the sidewalks. She came upon a small house and stopped for a moment, taking a whiff of the air—she was searching for a particular scent. She carried on down the street until suddenly she turned around and gazed up into the window of a two-story brick house.

I watched as she crept along the sidewalk leading up to the house. At first I thought she was going to knock on the door, but instead she burst through the window. My feet led me into the house without me willing them, and I followed her up a short flight of stairs. Down the hall, to the left, and into a small bedroom was a young boy sitting behind a desk reading a book.

"Hello, darling," Destiny said in the sweetest, most alluring voice she could manage.

Startled, the boy jumped up from his chair and opened his mouth to scream. Destiny was at his side at once, her hand tightly sealing his mouth.

"Please don't scream," she whispered. "I just want to play a little game with you is all. Do you like games?"

The boy nodded his head slowly.

"Good. This game is all about being as quiet as possible." She smiled against the warmth of his cheek. "I am going to remove my hand, but if you make the slightest sound you will lose the game. But, if you are a good little boy and don't make a peep, you will get a reward! Understand?"

Another slow nod.

"Perfect." She smiled again, removed her hand and studied the young boy. Her eyes tore away from the child and focused on the piece of paper lying on his desk. It was a childish drawing of a house surrounded by a lake and trees, with a scrawling of his signature.

Destiny gasped and pushed away from the boy. She looked frantic. "Your name ... " she whispered. "Alex?"

The boy opened his mouth to speak, then remembered the rule of the game and nodded yet again. He was trembling as she pulled his face into her hands. "I'm sorry...we can't play tonight. Don't tell anyone of this, understand?" Without another word, she crashed through his window and fled through the night.

"Malik ... I want to discuss something with you," I heard my mother speak as we appeared in a room lined with bookshelves built into the walls—every inch of which was filled top to bottom with books. A rounded crimson couch sat in the center of the room, upon which she and the other vampire sat.

"What is it?" he asked as he twirled a glass of thick red liquid in his hand.

"Do you ever intend to free me?"

"Why you would want to be free?" He glanced at her and frowned. "Do you not enjoy it here?"

"I would like to return to my home."

His expression darkened. "This is your home! This has always been your home, and shall always remain your home!"

"That's not true, Malik!" she shouted. "You can feed those lies to all the other slaves, but I know the truth! I was human once! I had a family. I had a daughter."

"Oh, is that what you want?" he asked with a playful smile. "I could have one brought to you—any child of your picking could be ours."

"No! That's not what I want!"

He sat down his glass and sighed. "You will never be pleased, will you? I give you everything you could ever need—your own living quarters, no chores but gathering food, better apparel than all the other slaves, and my undying love—and yet you still remain unhappy."

"I want my daughter back! That's all I want. You have all the slaves here that you could ever need; losing me won't hurt anything."

"Oh come now, I need you Destiny. I need you here." He stared longingly at her. "Do you not love me?"

"You beat me and lock me in the chambers. It isn't easy to love someone who treats you like a slave."

"If anyone knew the way I felt for you, a slave ... " Malik shook his head.

"If you loved me, you would make me your queen."

Malik almost laughed until he noticed how serious she was. "Are you suggesting that we wed?"

"Only if you love me," she replied. "Make me your queen and prove that you love me as much as you say you do, and take this slave title away from me."

He pondered her proposition for a moment, and then his lips formed into a wide smile. "I shall announce it at once."

"Wonderful," Destiny said with what I took to be a false smile as Malik kissed her.

After he left the room, my mother got to her feet and began pacing around the room. She was plotting something, but I wasn't sure what. Was this all a trick she was playing on him? Judging by the mischievous grin on her face, I was positive that she was.

Betrayal

It took me a few minutes to realize I had been pulled out of the visions, and Destiny was now speaking directly to me.

"Malik married me the following night, granting me the same power that he held. We dined on the finest of blood—the blood of children—and I grew stronger as time passed. He taught me how to hunt on my own, taught me how to be a true vampire and not just a slave. I grew to love him, but I was plagued with memories of a baby girl named Alexis, and I desired nothing more than to find her. He would become furious any time I mentioned you and tell me that he was my life now—none of the past mattered anymore. He would use his tricks of the mind on me, and for a time I would forget…but your face always haunted me…until I remembered again.

"Eventually not even his suppression could mask it, and I became obsessed with finding you. I spent hours dwelling on the vague pictures of you I saw in my mind—I saw the trailer, a brief glimpse of your father, and suddenly I remembered Willowshire. I remembered the night that Raziel killed me, and how Paul never came to find me.

"It was difficult to betray Malik after I had developed such strong feelings for him, but I had to find you. He offered on numerous occasions to find us an undead child to love as our own, but that was not what I wanted—I wanted *my* child. The daughter I remembered giving birth to, the one I remembered holding in my arms as she fell asleep ... and now here we are together at last."

"Alex—don't fall for this," Salem said harshly, distracting me from my mother's words. "She is corrupted—worse than Hannah was. She is tricking you, just as she tricked Malik. I can feel it."

"The boy is a liar, Alexis! I would never trick you, my only daughter—I sacrificed everything to find you!"

"Where is Paul?" I asked firmly, ignoring both of them.

"That doesn't matter, darling ... we are together now, nothing else matters."

"Tell me where Paul is, or I'll leave!"

"Oh, he's here," Destiny grinned maniacally, "gagged and bound in the bathroom."

"What? Is he hurt?"

"No. At least not yet ... " The grin never faltered. "You see, Alex, your father made me a promise that he would always protect you from this secret life of hunting vampires. He swore that you would live an ordinary life, no matter what—yet here you are, without the beating heart I left you with."

"It's in my blood to be a hunter. I would have found out eventually anyway."

"Not if Paul had kept his promise!" she shrieked and leapt up from the bed.

Her fist slammed into the door to the master bathroom, knocking it off its hinges, and she dragged my father out. His hands were tied behind his back and a thick layer of tape sealed his mouth shut. She thrust him onto the ground in front of the bed and I heard a faint whimper escape him.

"Don't do anything you'll regret," I said and jumped off of the bed.

"Why should you want him to live, Alex? He betrayed us both. It is his fault, all of it! Him and his damned hunting! I wish I had never met him, or that I would have left with you when I had the chance. He took us away from one another Alex! He didn't even try! Oh, and I pried out of him what's happened since. He didn't want to talk, but I can be pretty persuasive when I need to be."

She slowly licked at a bloody gash across Paul's cheekbone before continuing. "He told me about giving you up to that Janet woman and her pathetic husband Desmond. Pawning them off as your parents because he didn't want to raise you."

"You shut your mouth about them! Janet was more of a mom to me than you will ever be."

"Is that a way to talk to your mother?"

"You're not my mother!"

She smiled. Her eyes turned a brilliant crimson, and she lunged at Paul.

"No! You can't blame him for this!" I shouted as she pinned him to the ground. "He thought you were gone for good—he's been devastated over the loss of the love of his life, and tried to protect me for as long as he could! Giving me up was the only way!"

That was enough to grab her attention at least temporarily.

"Even so, he eventually told you. He brought you into this world of blood, and look what it has done to you. It is his fault that we are like this Alex."

"It wasn't exactly Paul who first told Alexis," Salem chimed in.

"Ah, so this pretty boy here is the one who tainted my baby?" she growled and approached Salem, leaving Paul on the floor.

"She would have discovered the truth eventually on her own," he replied, not even a hint of fear shown on his face. "Your daughter is more than she appears."

"What does he mean?" she asked, turning briefly to stare at me.

With a sigh, I transformed before my mother showing her what I truly was. Her face drew a blank as she marveled at me. "You ... you are a raven?"

"Yes." I nodded, "I was born to hunt, whether I wanted to or not."

"This can't be!" she cried. "Not my baby! You were innocent, pure and beautiful ... I was meant to protect you ... nurture you ... keep you away from the monsters of this world ... "

"Unfortunately, you are one of the monsters," I said and lowered my eyes for a brief second. "Salem might be a vampire, and so am I now ... but we do not murder people."

"Don't you dare call your mother a monster!" she screamed.

"But you are a monster, and a murderer. Ever since I first learned of you, I've been longing to meet you, wishing I could have known you, thinking you had died ... and now, I have to do my duty in life and rid the world of one more monster, mother or not."

"Alex?" Salem said in shock. "No ... There has to be something else you can do. Something we can do. Maybe she can change...like...like Hannah!"

I shook my head. I wished I could cry. I wanted to feel the warmth of fresh tears coursing down my face—but none came. Not because I didn't care. I did care. I wanted nothing more than to be reunited with my mother, to grow to know and love her, but she was long gone. The Destiny my father had fallen in love with was gone, and all that was left was an empty shell of who she once was. She was not Destiny Waldron anymore. I had to see her as what she truly was—a corrupted, insane, murderous vampire, beyond the point of help.

"She's gone, Salem. She can't be saved. You and I both know it's true."

Paul kicked around on the floor with intent to trip me, but I was too fast. I moved out of his reach and stared down at him with disbelief.

"This isn't the woman you love, dad! You have to know that."

He closed his eyes and looked away.

"I'm sorry, dad," I whispered.

"You think you can kill me?" Destiny laughed mockingly. "You're just a hunter with no weapon."

"I am a weapon," I disagreed. "Salem, leave. Please."

"I won't leave you with her."

"Leave! I don't want to hurt you, too!"

Without another word, he exited the room, glancing back once to look me directly in the eyes.

Irony

Destiny cackled and leapt at me, slamming me into my father's brown dresser. My back ached temporarily, but it wasn't enough to prevent me from attacking back. I spun around, my talons extracted and my mouth open in preparation to shriek, but she was faster than I had imagined. Her foot met my side and sent me clambering toward the floor. Sticking out a hand, I grasped the edge of the bed and stopped myself from falling.

"You don't want to fight me, Alex," she said in a hypnotic voice. "Let's live together and be the happy family we were always meant to be."

"I wish we could," I whispered before letting out a shrill shriek. She cowered with her hands over her ears, and I immediately took advantage by leaping towards her. As I swung to sink my claws into her, she caught my arm by the wrist. Smiling up at me, she started to plead again.

"You could come back with me, Alex. You could be the daughter to Malik and me. We can still be together, like this, forever. Come on sweetie, please?"

"Never!"

"Wrong answer!" With one swift motion, Destiny twisted the wrist she was holding, snapping it completely.

The pain in my arm was immense. I had thought I would feel little pain as a vampire, but I had been very wrong. The snapped bones sent a wave of sickening pain up my arm, and I collapsed down onto my knees.

"We could have been together again, Alexis. One big happy family. I could have shown you the world, and you could have had anything you ever desired at your fingertips."

"No…no I couldn't. My dad…my friends…Salem. I would never give any of them up, for anything!"

"Oh Alex, baby. You will come with me, one way or another, you know. Even if I have to let you live the life of a slave for a while like I did. You will come with me."

"I'll never go with you. I'd rather die!"

"Oh come now, don't be dramatic. What did this Janet woman teach you anyway? Certainly didn't do too great of a job, I guess, huh? Here, I will give you a choice. If you come with me now, without a fight, I will let your dad and your friends live. I'll even let your little vampire lover come with us if I really must. However, if you refuse…not only will I make you go, but I will kill them."

"No…you can't… I won't let you."

"Oh, there's nothing you can do about it. It's an easy choice, really. Come with me and they can all go on about their boring, short little lives. Refuse and I will kill them all, and it will be slow. I'll start by draining your dad here of every drop." She kicked him lightly in the leg before continuing, "Then I will find my way to your little friend's house that your poor daddy told me about. Your old house, right? What was that boy's name? Jim? John? …*Jason*? I think I may do something extravagant with them. Maybe take a bath in their blood as you watch. You were all for the dramatics, right?" She laughed.

"Jason..." I whispered to myself.

"Well, what do you say? Come with mommy?"

What choice did I have? I couldn't just leave with her, and pretend nothing ever happened. I couldn't exactly leave my friends to die either though. If only I had been strong enough to beat her. Maybe there was still hope, after all...Salem had to be somewhere close by to help.

I looked around for him, but saw nothing. Why had I told him to leave? I looked out the window, hoping to see him there, but only saw darkness.

"Salem!" I shouted with as much hope and surprise as I could muster. Maybe she would believe that I had seen him.

It worked! As Destiny turned to look for Salem out the window I had been staring at, I seized the moment: As loud as I could, I cawed. As she crumbled onto the floor, I had no time to waste. I stood up...ignoring the pain in my arm for a moment...and jumped over to the dresser with my dad's silver crossbow on top of it. I grabbed the weapon, rolled carefully across the bed and cawed again before Destiny had the opportunity to regain her senses.

This was never a position I ever foresaw myself in—standing in front of my mother, a weapon aimed at her chest with intent to kill. But what other choice did I have? How ironic was it that it was my *destiny* to kill her? For a brief moment, I contemplated giving her a chance like Salem had for Hannah, but I knew it would be a bad idea. She was far too gone, and she would never be the same. Besides, she deserved to die...just thinking of all the people she had killed over the past years made me sick. She even admitted to drinking the blood of children. I shuddered.

I shut my eyes, pulled the trigger and tried to block out the cries of agony protruding from the mouth of the woman who, despite the monster she was, traveled the world to find me because, deep down, she remembered me, she loved me and couldn't live without me. If I could change the world to be how I believed it was before I met Salem, would I? I wasn't sure. Maybe it would have been better had I always thought Janet was my real mother, and if I had ended up with Jason instead of Salem. No. This was my life now. *This was my destiny.*

Once my eyes were opened, I dropped the crossbow to the floor and focused on the limp body of my mother on the floor. It hurt to look at her, but I wouldn't let it end like this. I knelt beside her cold, dead corpse and kissed her lightly on the cheek.

"I love you, mom ... " I whispered. "I am so sorry it had to end this way." I swept my hand across her eyelids, and they fell shut—forever.

Paul was wriggling on the floor beside the end of the bed, trying to get himself loose from the rope binding his arms. I barely noticed his presence in the room during the fight against Destiny, despite his constant muffled groans and screams beneath the tape. If only I could have left then, I may have saved myself a lot of pain, but instead I ran to his side and cut through the bindings with my talons. I switched forms and plucked the tape from his mouth. He screamed and rubbed his mouth, then without any warning, he slammed his fist into my jaw.

"What the hell was that for?!" I screamed, holding my face.

"You just killed your mother! My wife!" he yelled.

"Calm down, dad! That thing was NOT your wife!"

"She could have gotten better," he insisted and ran to her side. He held her hand tightly in his own, and I saw a tear fall and hit her cheek. "Oh, Destiny … "

"Dad, you have to understand…she was going to kill you!" I shrieked, avoiding getting too close to him.

"I could have convinced her not to … somehow. I just know it. My Destiny was still in there, under all this…"

"No. That's just how you wish things would have turned out. We both know that she is not the woman you loved."

"You're wrong!" he yelled furiously, picked up the crossbow and scrambled to his feet. "She would have listened to me, realized I didn't break my promise, and with time, everything would be the same again!"

"Face it, dad," I pleaded, eying the crossbow anxiously. "The truth is…mom did die that day, so long ago."

"No…I know the truth," he growled. "Where is that filthy little vampire shit of yours anyway?!"

"I-I don't know," I stuttered. Paul pushed me aside and stormed out of the room, down the hall and began frantically searching through the trailer. "What are you doing?!"

I chased after him through each room, and then he spotted the front door hanging wide open and ran down the stairs.

Salem was leaning against my car, staring up toward the twinkling stars in the dark sky. I watched him turn around to face us, "Paul?" he said. "Is it over?"

"Oh, it's about to be," Paul snarled. "I never took the time to think about it before, but it all makes sense now!"

Arching a brow, Salem eyed the crossbow in my father's hand and frowned. "I don't know what you are talking about, Paul. You must be mistaken."

"No, I'm not mistaken, Salem. You never should have come here. That's what led to all of this. *You.*"

"Dad! Stop! You're just upset. You need to relax," I begged and grabbed onto his arm.

He thrust me aside and I hit the stair banister, falling to my knees. "Stay out of this Alex. You ought to have realized it by now, too. Salem is the reason behind everything! If he had never come here, Raziel wouldn't have been in Colorado eighteen years ago! Your mother would still be alive, sane and healthy, and so would you!"

"What? That's crazy!" I yelled as I pulled myself to my feet. "Any other vampire could have killed mom just the same, or turned me. All of this could have played out identical with or without Salem. What happened happened…and there is nothing anyone could have ever done to change it."

Paul shook his head. He appeared almost as demented as Destiny had. "Destiny…fate … call it whatever you want. All I know is this bastard owes me for all the pain he has caused."

The crossbow shook in his unsteady hand as he lifted it and pointed toward Salem.

"You're making a huge mistake, dad!" I shouted, leaping toward him. The sound of the trigger going off reached my ears as I tackled him to the ground.

It was going to be okay. He had bad aim. He never hit the target. Salem would be okay. Then why did I refuse to look up? Why was I so afraid that he hadn't missed? Why didn't I hear Salem? Not even a scream …

Hesitantly, I looked up. I saw the Alero, glittering slightly under the moonlight. I saw the Jeep Wrangler parked beside it. Where was Salem?

Goodbyes Are Never Easy

I tore the crossbow away from Paul, elbowed him hard in the head and left him unconscious in the gravel. Climbing to my feet wasn't easy, I felt like I couldn't move—I was afraid to move. Then I spotted him, sprawled on the ground beside my car.

"Salem?" I said as I approached him. My voice was shaky and sounded unusual to me. "Salem, please ... "

Kneeling down beside him, I found the arrow embedded in his chest. The blood soaked through his white T-shirt and formed a pool beneath his body. He wasn't breathing, but that didn't mean anything ... did it?

"Salem ... " I cried, "No, no, no...this can't be happening!"

I shook him, but he didn't react. "Please, Salem!" I frantically tore at his shirt, ripping through the fabric to reveal just where the arrow had struck. It was close ... it was too close.

Still no response. "This ought to get your attention ... " I said hoarsely and ripped the arrow out of his chest, but he didn't move. "Come on ... Salem ... "

I laid my head against his abdomen, wishing the tears would come so that I could relieve myself of the anguish I felt.

"Paul is unconscious, if you're pretending, you can stop now ... please ... " I begged.

"That was a close call," he whispered and pulled me into his arms. I fought the urge to slap him for scaring me, but I was too relieved to care about anything else but the sound of his voice and feel of his touch.

"We need to get out of here," I said, eying Paul's body. "We need to go to the Victorian, get what we can, get Hannah and leave Willowshire."

His brow furrowed as he stared at me. "But Alex, your friends are here ... your family ... "

"My family wants to kill you—and quite possibly me as well!"

"And what about your friends?" he asked.

"They'll be okay without me. They'll probably forget all about me eventually anyway. Jason has his new girlfriend and Karen...Karen's almost like a stranger to me now ... "

"No, they wouldn't. You and I both know that. You have left a great impact on their lives. You need them, and they need you. Paul will come to his senses eventually."

"I'm not so sure he will, Salem." I frowned. "You weren't there. You didn't see him...hear him. I think Destiny dying put him over the edge. We need to leave, even if it's only for a little while ... "

"Where will we go?"

"Anywhere! We'll just get in the car and drive until we find somewhere we like ... we can tell everyone that we're going on vacation or something. It'll give Paul some time to set himself straight ... I hope."

Salem stared into my eyes and pondered the idea. I heard Paul grunt and glanced in his direction. He was still unconscious, but I didn't know how long it would last. "Okay. We will do it. Let's go home. We will tell Richard that he can stay in the Victorian for as long as he likes. Then you will pack up your laptop, I will find Hannah, and we will leave—temporarily. You will send letters or e-mails to Jason, Mitchell and Karen and inform them that we have left for a vacation and that we will be back sometime soon … just promise to keep in touch with them."

"Deal," I replied with a slight smile. "Now, let's get out of here before he wakes up."

"Alexis..?"

"Yeah?"

"Your arm…" he pointed at the mangled mess of bone that I had somehow forgotten about during everything that had happened.

"Oh, right." I closed my eyes and concentrated on my arm. This time I was prepared with some relaxing thoughts. I thought about my mom…the only *real* mom I had ever known. I thought about Janet. About being chased through the yard of the old house with a water hose on a hot summer day. About being tickled and laughing. Memories of a childhood when everything was so much simpler. Before I could imagine the events of this night, even in my wildest dreams.

I opened my eyes, and all traces of the injury was gone.

"Okay, let's go."

When we arrived at the house, I was relieved to find that my grandfather was asleep in the guest room, and I got to avoid any awkward goodbyes. I scrawled a simple note on a piece of paper Salem summoned for me and explained what happened and requested that he try to convince Paul that he was mistaken. Hannah was out hunting but returned moments after we showed up. She was furious upon discovering Paul nearly killed her half-brother and at first was keen on the idea of going after him. After a bit of calming, she finally agreed that it was wisest to leave. She didn't want to be tempted back to her old ways, even if he 'deserved it' as she put it.

I unplugged my laptop, and reflected on the day that Jason had given it to me. I took the computer to the car, along with my volume of Edgar Allan Poe's stories, sat them in the backseat and sat down. Taking my cell phone out, I dialed Jason's number and was unsurprised that it went directly to voice mail. The beep came and I sighed.

"Jason ... it's Alex. I am happy for you and Eila, really—you deserve to have someone like her in your life. Salem and I are going out of town for a while; I don't know when we'll be back. Tell Karen and Mitchell for me ... I love you all and will miss you," I paused for a moment, and then added in a hoarse voice as the words fought to come out, "Goodbye ... "

Hannah had practically begged to take the driver's seat, and I happily agreed. It was nice having someone else drive for a change. Salem and I sat together in the back-seat, my head leaning comfortably against his shoulder as I skimmed through the book he had created for me out of the plain black leather diary Janet had given me. My makeshift bookmark was still in pristine condition, regardless how many times I had shifted it between different sections throughout the book as I read. It struck me that I was almost finished with the entire volume, and my eyes trailed eagerly down the last few pages as we passed by the sign saying we were leaving Willowshire.

Salem glanced down at the book. "You have made a lot of progress," he commented.

Turning the final page of the book, I flinched and pulled back as the paper sliced along my index finger. It was sort of funny, paper cuts still hurting even as a vampire. As I smiled, I noted the drop of blood splotched onto the aged papers, and before I had the chance to say anything to Salem, I noticed something else. The pages transformed right before my eyes from the words of Edgar Allan Poe to a scrawled text that was hardly decipherable. Flipping back through the previous pages, I noticed that all of the words Salem had magically summoned into the journal were vanishing and becoming replaced by this unfamiliar text.

"Salem..." I muttered nearly inaudibly, "what...what's going on?"

"This must not have been just an ordinary journal after all..." he replied and glanced at the words developing on the page. "It looks to be an ancient journal belonging to someone who was very well versed in the ways of vampires..."

"What gives you that idea?" Hannah asked from the driver's seat and looked back at us.

"The writer mentions them on nearly every page that Alex has turned through," he answered as he flipped through some more of the pages. "And keep your eye on the road, Hannah."

"What do you think this means?" I asked, staring at the words as they evolved on each page Salem turned to.

"I think it is going to prove to be more useful to you than Janet ever imagined..."

The End

Thank you very much for reading Hybrid!

I know your time is valuable, and I sincerely thank you for finishing my novel. If you would take a brief moment to return to an online book retailer and leave a review it would be much appreciated!

Reviews help new readers find my work and accurately decide if the book is for them as well as provide valuable feedback for my future writing.

Also, if you enjoyed the book, please be sure to tell a friend and check out the rest of the books in the Nevermore series!

Thank you again, and be sure to sign up to my mailing list to be alerted of new releases, giveaways, and more!
http://www.kaylapoe.com/mailing-list

About the Author

KA Poe lives in Arizona with her husband and daughter. Someday she hopes to travel the world and live life to the fullest she possibly can. Writing has always been her passion. When she isn't writing she spends a lot of time reading, playing computer games, browsing the web, and spending time with her family. She has a vivid imagination, an eccentric personality and collects colorful socks.

To learn more about the author please visit her website at:
http://www.kaylapoe.com

Find her on Facebook at:
http://www.facebook.com/kaylapoe

Follow her on Twitter at:
http://www.twitter.com/KAPoeAuthor

Or e-mail her at:
kayla.a.poe@gmail.com

Also please sign up for the newsletter to be notified of new releases!
http://www.kaylapoe.com/mailing-list

Also By

Be sure to check these other novels by K.A. Poe!

THE NEVERMORE SERIES
Twin Souls
Hybrid
Sacrifice
Destiny

THE FOREVERMORE SERIES
Kismet
Catalyst

THE ANI'MARI SAGA
Ephemeral
Evanescent

THE AVARIAL TRILOGY
The King's Hourglass
The Phantom's Gift

DARIUS (Serial)
Through the Rift